Sheer Bliss

Sheer Bliss

A CREOLE JOURNEY ⟫⟪

Michela A. Calderaro

The University of the West Indies Press

Jamaica • Barbados • Trinidad and Tobago

The University of the West Indies Press
7A Gibraltar Hall Road, Mona
Kingston 7, Jamaica
www.uwipress.com

A catalogue record of this book is available
from the National Library of Jamaica.

ISBN: 978-976-640-813-8 (paper)
978-976-640-814-5 (Kindle)
978-976-640-815-2 (ePub)

The University of the West Indies Press has no responsibility for the persistence or accuracy of URLs for external or third-party Internet websites referred to in this publication and does not guarantee that any content on such websites is, or will remain, accurate or appropriate.

Cover illustration by Alexander Zass
Cover and book design by Robert Harris
Set in Dante 11/15 x 24

Printed in the United States of America

Contents

Illustrations

Preface

When I first read Eliot Bliss's novels, *Saraband* and *Luminous Isle*, I could not imagine I would be embarking on a twenty-year quest in her footsteps. I was simply driven by my curiosity and puzzled by the fact that there was no information to be found about her writings nor her life. I could not even confirm such details as her birth name, Eileen Nora, or why she had changed it to Eliot.

Most of my academic work until then had been dedicated to carrying on research and writing critical analyses of works by British modernist writers and, later, Caribbean writers, as well as teaching courses on lesbian and feminist theories and writers, strictly focusing on textual or historical theories, always trying to distance myself from the writers' lives. As a celebrated writer's grandchild once argued, "You have his books, why probe his life?"[1]

Sheer Bliss follows a different path altogether. I found myself involved in research without knowing where it would lead me. Soon enough I realized I could not analyse Bliss's works and shed light on the circumstances and social context surrounding their writing without describing my personal quest and the meetings with people she knew.

This book, then, is more like a diary of my years-long attempt to bring Eliot Bliss out of undeserved obscurity. It is not, nor does it claim to be, a traditional biography. Indeed, it is not a biography at all, as I don't see my role here as that of a biographer or a historian. It is, rather, a researcher's report of her quest to get to know more about a talented writer – written as a chronology of my finds, or, in some cases, of failures to find what I was seeking to uncover, rather than a straightforward chronology of Bliss's life.

---

1 Stephen James Joyce, Joyce's grandson, comment during the eleventh International James Joyce Symposium, Venice, 1988.

And so, since the unexpected "encounter" with Eliot Bliss changed my perspective as a critic and forced me to adopt a new approach, the present work is also a testimony to this change, as well as to the way it affected both my personal and my academic life.

I was bound to work on Eliot Bliss during my time away from my day job at the University of Trieste, and so my own family became involved in the search. Personal friends and acquaintances became instrumental in my search as well, providing places to stay or work when I was away from home.

In my "diary", I incorporated articles I had previously written about Eliot Bliss, because they were part of the search, part of my attempt to find more manuscripts, more poems, more answers. Also, I chose to keep the original version of the various documents I quote (Eliot Bliss's diaries and letters, or letters by other people), even where words are misspelled or grammatical errors are found, because they provide a glimpse of their writers' state of mind.

Bliss's "mystery" stirred my curiosity and drove me to embark on a journey through an uncharted territory which often felt endless and fruitless – uncharted because her writings posed a complex interpretative challenge. They can be labelled as belonging to different "schools". While not appearing to belong in any specific genre, they actually belong by right in quite a number of them.

They are modernist, in that they follow in the steps of such writers as Joseph Conrad and Ford Madox Ford, but also Henry James, who stood at the centre of the transition from the old order towards a new way of writing. Not much action is shown, and her protagonists too are the expressions of a society on the brink of disaster, stubbornly resisting novelty and oblivious to the wind of change destined to destroy their world. They are feminist, because her new way of writing is applied to portray Dorothy Richardson's female way to self-discovery. They are lesbian, since they lead towards a lesbian literary tradition that was then still in its germinal stage. They are full expressions of a creole identity, and constitute, especially *Luminous Isle*, a courageous endeavour to describe the reality of pre-decolonization white society.

Using the experimental tools of modernist fiction, Bliss exposed the delicate issue of creoleness, the interplay of race and gender, the impact of colonial heritage and the tragedy endured during decolonization. Though her name and work are little known, her mentors were the most influential figures of London's modernist, feminist and lesbian circles: Dorothy Richardson, Anna Wickham and Natalie Clifford Barney. Studying her work, then, is certain to lead to a better understanding of the influences of modernism on the complex nature of creole women's writing – of which, I strongly believe, she is the clearest expression. Her writings indeed reflect, on one hand, the tension between the community and culture of her birth, and on the other, the community and culture of exile, as well as their effect on her individuality. Eliot Bliss's work bears witness to this tension and to the feeling of being *different* within one's own community.

In this sense, Bliss was a real historian of her times, chronicling events and history without any romantic or sentimental distortion. The strong and straightforward criticism of white, racist life in the colonies, as expressed by the description of certain characters in her novels, especially her mother's, was bound to raise outrage among readers; but she did not change a single phrase exposing such racism, or revealing her attraction towards a black island girl.

During my journey I had the fortune of meeting and becoming friends with Patricia Allan-Burns, Bliss's lifelong companion. Our encounter led not only to an unexpected and beautiful friendship and the rescue of precious unpublished material, but also to the discovery of Bliss's unknown talent for painting.

Pictures related to Eliot Bliss and Patricia Allan-Burns together with some of Bliss's delicate and beautiful Jamaica drawings and watercolours are published here for the first time.

CHAPTER 1

The Meeting

Bishop's Stortford

15 April 2004

She was standing right in front of me, at the end of the street. She seemed to have appeared suddenly out of nowhere – out of an opening in the tall brick wall that was covered with rosemary. She was leaning, but just slightly, on a stick, and staring at me.

"Here you are. Come on in."

I had been walking up and down the street that morning looking for 152 Plaw Hatch Close, all the time dismissing the half-hidden opening in the crumbling wall.

A cold sweat was running down my back. The light drizzle had covered my glasses with a watery film. I felt uncomfortable. Uttering some sort of excuse for being late, I moved towards her and entered. She was already crossing a garden, then turned her head and looked at me.

"I told you, the house was next to the school."

She led the way, waving her stick and naming all the flowers and plants that she herself had planted over the years and was still taking care of. The sheen on my glasses made every petal and leaf shine. I felt as if I had entered Frances Hodgson Burnett's *Secret Garden*.

I followed her past the garden into a small entrance to a narrow, short corridor. The door on my left was to Eliot's room, I would be told later. And two other doors on my right led to the bathroom and to Sylvia's room. Past the corridor was the living room, and to its right, a small kitchen.

"You sit there." She pointed at a chair next to a bed in the living room, her bed for the last forty-five years. Piled on a little table were letters, pictures and a folder. She sat in front of me, in an armchair; next to her was another small table, crammed with an ashtray, a spray for asthma, a pile of new books. She followed my eyes while I took in the room.

"I like reading, keeping informed. So, what would you like to know?" Her voice was like a rumble, a distant rumble, and she was looking at me with piercing, unflinching, light blue eyes.

"I'm a researcher, as I mentioned. I've read Ms Bliss's novels and would like to know more about her, her life, her work. I would actually like just to *know* her, since nothing has been written so far, and I like her books," I explained.

A smile finally illuminated her face. She must have been striking at nineteen, in 1933, when she first met Eliot Bliss.

"I would like to know Eliot through your eyes," I said.

"I'll make some coffee, or would you like something else?"

"Coffee . . . perfect."

She stood up and disappeared into the kitchen; I didn't dare stir. She came back and handed me a cup of coffee – sugar, I realized, was on the table in front of me. I sipped, burning my throat in reverent silence, already spellbound.

She sat back in her armchair, very quietly.

"I was an art student . . . very young. My father insisted that if I take up this scholarship, at London Central School of Arts. . . . To be quite honest with you, dear, I was sort of . . . in a world I had rarely ever known. I was brought up very strictly, you'd say. I mean, we weren't allowed out unchaperoned, and, you see, I was with Patience and Eliot at the time when they were parting, and I didn't know a thing, I didn't understand, it was only later that one realized . . ."

I was breathless; she was letting me enter her life.

It had taken me six years to find her.

BEFORE

New York
13 July 1998

It was a hot Monday, we were having lunch, as we had done in the past, at one of my favourite restaurants, the Knickerbocker Bar and Grill.

"You look good!" I said. It was true, though he was dying. "I need your help, I don't know whom to ask, and in a few days I'll be going back to Italy. So, Jim, you *must* help me."

Jim Tuttleton would die a few months later of pancreatic cancer. He had been my mentor and friend at New York University, one of the brightest minds around. I had flown to New York especially to see him but pretended I was on a scholarship for some sort of research. I could only stay for a week.

Actually, as often happens, while pretending to carry on an imaginary research project, I had stumbled on a real literary puzzle.

"Have you ever heard of a writer called Eliot Bliss? I searched everywhere: Library, MLA, Internet, Britannica – there's no mention of her. I searched the catalogue at Bobst,[1] but even there I couldn't discover anything! I found this book in one of my favourite known-only-to-the-initiated second-hand bookstores. It's a second edition." I handed him the book, *Saraband*, a tattered soft-cover I'd likely have ignored and left on its dusty shelf were it not for the word "Jamaica" on its back cover, noting the author's place of birth, and followed by the detail that she had been friends with Anna Wickham, Jean Rhys and Dorothy Richardson.

"Have you asked George Thompson[2] at Bobst to help you? He remembers exactly where each book is!" he suggested with a hearty laugh.

"I haven't had much time to contact him."

"Is the book any good?"

"Oh, yes! Sounds a bit like James, or even Ford, the description of a society that is crumbling. But it also gives you a strange feeling, as if there's more to it than a mere autobiographical novel, the way they describe it on the book cover."

"I have no idea. . . . Well, you've got your little mystery to solve." And he smiled. "Shall we have lunch Wednesday, and discuss a line of investigation? Same place?"

I would never see him again after that lunch at Knickerbocker Bar and Grill. He was hospitalized the next day.

---

1   New York University Library.

2   George Thompson, *A Documentary History of the African Theatre* (Evanston, IL: Northwestern University Press, 1998). The book explores the story of the first all-black theatre company in the United States, founded in 1821 in New York by William Alexander Brown.

Venice
1999

Saraband sat on my shelves for quite a while, among other books by Caribbean authors. I couldn't find Bliss's second novel, *Luminous Isle*, mentioned on the book cover, though I searched for it in many bookstores and libraries.

Since seeking anything connected to Bliss bore few, if any, fruits besides frustration, I was soon distracted by other, already planned, projects, and by my workload at the University of Trieste. I was working on a paper on Ford Madox Ford at the time, for a conference to be held in Münster in June 1999, and was thrilled at the prospect. Ford had been my ongoing "love affair", and I was looking forward to the pleasure of mixing with old friends: the group of lively, enthusiastic and knowledgeable scholars of the Ford Madox Ford Society.

Thinking about what to write (Punctuation in modernist fiction, perhaps?), I was looking for something physical to do that would not interfere with my Fordian frame of mind. I decided to put my desk and my shelves in order: "my" part of the studio I share with my husband.

On the floor lay a pile of books I had collected during my tours at Argosy, the Strand, Gotham Bookmart, Octagon Books, and other favourite old-book dealers. Next to it another pile: articles I had gathered the year before in New York and hadn't had the time to catalogue properly. Because of Jean Rhys's liaison with Ford Madox Ford, I had begun reading her novels and come to appreciate her style, and actually fell in love with the Caribbean landscape. I wanted to write about her work, and all those piled articles and books were to constitute the critical background to my own analysis of her novels.

Among them was a book by Evelyn O'Callaghan,[3] a scholar whose works I had always admired. I was flipping distractedly through its pages, when my eye fell on something that made me stop, startled. One of the chapters dealt with white creole women writers, and three names stood out: Jean Rhys, Phyllis Shand Allfrey and Eliot Bliss.

---

3   Evelyn O'Callaghan, *Woman Version: Theoretical Approaches to West Indian Fiction by Women* (New York: St. Martin's Press, 1993), 28–35. The chapter devoted to Jean Rhys, Phyllis Shand Allfrey and Eliot Bliss is a revised version of "The Outsider's Voice: White Creole Women Novelists in the Caribbean Literary Tradition," *Journal of West Indian Literature* 1, no. 1 (1986): 74–88.

The piles would remain unattended and my plans to impose some order postponed indefinitely.

I had, a few years before, written a brief article about Phyllis Shand Allfrey, and then devoted myself completely to what I thought would have been my book on Rhys – which never took off. But here was Bliss's name. The chapter did not say much on Bliss's life and briefly analysed only one book, *Luminous Isle,* the one I had not read.

Again, she was mentioned in connection with Jean Rhys, with whom, I was to discover, she was very close. I decided to start with the name indexes in all books about Rhys in my possession; later I would search connections to poet Anna Wickham and to Dorothy Richardson. First, I picked up *The Letters of Jean Rhys*, edited by Francis Wyndham. A note on a letter from Jean Rhys to Peggy Kirkaldy,[4] who was also a friend of Dorothy Richardson, read: "Eliot (real name Eileen) Bliss was born in Kingston, Jamaica, and educated at a Highgate convent and University College, London. She published two novels: *Saraband* (1931) and *Luminous Isle* (1934). She got to know Jean in 1937, through an introduction from Horace Gregory, and used to visit the Tilden-Smiths at Paulton's Square where Jean would cook her 'delicious West Indian meals'."[5]

Now I knew her *real* name. The information contained in the letter and in the note, though scarce, added to what I had learned so far. Then I looked at Carole Angier's *Jean Rhys,* where I found a reference to Eliot Bliss, and to the fact that the two were friends. Her relationship with Jean Rhys seemed to me, at the time, the most promising. From what I read, the intellectual connection between the two women was stronger than what one could infer from the vague references to Bliss in Rhys's collection of letters. Eliot was a good friend indeed, I would discover. Their friendship, which began in 1936, was important to both throughout their lives. Eliot travelled to America, and then to Hertfordshire, but the correspondence went on even after the war. She was

---

4   Peggy (1894–1958), whose full name was Margaret Mansfield Jacks, married Tom Kirkaldy, and took his family name. She was a socialite, known in literary circles, whose friends included the most famous artists of the period, not only Jean Rhys and Dorothy Richardson, but also Elizabeth Bowen, Osbert Sitweel and Denton Welch. Her parties were always crowded with writers, painters and scholars, and her salon was the place to be and promote one's work.

5   Francis Wyndham and Diana Melly, eds., *The Letters of Jean Rhys* (London: André Deutsch, 1984), 35–36.

always sympathetic and understanding, especially during what Carole Angier defines as Rhys's "very drunken moments": "She would rail at Eliot for being an 'unfeeling aristocrat', accuse her of belonging to the snobs and prigs and respectable people. [. . .] But here was the key to their friendship, and to why it ended only because Eliot left for America: Eliot didn't mind. 'Jean didn't mean it' [. . .]. 'She wasn't attacking me, she was attacking the world.' I'd seen it before, in other artists. This was the sort of understanding Jean needed."[6]

Carole Angier stresses the importance of "Eliot's glimpse of Jean in 1937 [. . .]. Without it our picture [of Jean] would be different, and darker".[7] But I could not find any description of Eliot: her figure, like her writings, had been overshadowed by her more famous contemporaries. I wondered why, and was saddened to think of such a talented writer completely forgotten, of her books being out of print; it felt as if she had never existed.

I *had* to know more about her; I *had* to read *Luminous Isle*.

I could not find the book in any library within my reach, so I got in touch with Alessandra Zorzi, librarian at Ca' Foscari, University of Venice, and asked for advice. She could get the book for me, she said, but I had to read it at the library; I could take notes, but photocopying large parts was forbidden.

⋙⋘

Waiting for *Luminous Isle* to arrive, I began reading Dorothy Richardson's biography and works, as I had never read anything by her before. She had been influential and admired in her time, and used to surround herself with a court of young promising writers. A few surprises were in store for me in her *Collected Letters*.

In the collection, Eliot Bliss's name is briefly mentioned, with a condescending tone, in two letters to Peggy Kirkaldy. The first is dated 30 October 1940:

> Dear Peggy,
>   A hurried line. my first thought was to evade by saying that my East A. friends [. . .] had gone to Jamaica. E.B. [Eliot Bliss] who is a great friend of Anna Wickham, has been so to speak, running after me for years. This, for me, is a

---

6   Carole Angier, *Jean Rhys* (London: André Deutsch, 1990), 362.
7   Ibid., 361.

mystery, for I cannot like her. I fail, however I may try. Lately, for some years, she has been in one difficulty after another [. . .]. Her little friend[,] a scholarship artist, now in commercial art, I do like. I leave it to you. If you so instruct me, (just a card) I'll do as proposed above. She has quality, & a sheer fundamental integrity I can't quite name or fathom. Too good for me perhaps. But there is something that always "puts me off". She appears to make friends (where?) she goes & to escape, at the eleventh hour from her difficulties.[8]

A footnote by the editor explained that the scholarship artist "would be Patricia Allan-Burns, Eliot Bliss's companion for fifty years". She had a female companion then; "her little friend", Richardson had called her, so I guessed she was probably younger than Eliot.

The following letter to Peggy Kirkaldy, dated 8 December 1940, gave me a better picture of Eliot Bliss and Patricia Allan-Burns. Richardson's patronizing tone is more evident than in the first letter:

The little girl, met as a hovering scout when, years ago on first going to see E.B., [. . .] who was laid up with a damaged leg (she seems subject to leg accidents) I was wandering in search of their warren amongst tall irregular numbered grey old Maida Vale houses-turned-tenements, charmed me at once slinking shyly up & putting a small hand on my arm, looking herself more lost than I. But throughout the meeting I felt her not liking me for not adoring E.B. I can't, as they say, make her out, Alan revolts utterly, & yet we both feel aware of a certain engaging strength & quiet confidence, even in the worst of vicissitudes. Their present plight is distressing & I am wondering whether their holding back from your lovely plan for them is not simply a matter of clo'[thes]![9]

So they must have been facing a difficult period, and Eliot had asked for help – perhaps she needed some contacts in the literary world – but Richardson's answer had been cold, to say the least, showing a strong distaste, an uncalled-for contempt.

---

8   Gloria G. Fromm, ed., *Windows on Modernism: Selected Letters of Dorothy Richardson* (Athens: University of Georgia Press, 1995), 409–10; brackets in the original.

9   Ibid., 412.

❄❄❄

When *Luminous Isle* arrived, through an interlibrary loan, I sat in the library for hours, taking notes, copying paragraphs on my yellow pad with my soft pencils.

Eliot Bliss wrote *Luminous Isle* in 1934, but the book I was holding in my hands was a second edition, published by Virago Press, just like the copy of *Saraband* I had bought in New York. I had hoped to be able to read the first edition, but I was happy all the same.

My hunch regarding Richardson's coldness was confirmed by Eliot Bliss herself, as quoted in the book's introduction.

Anna Wickham, the poet, had drawn Bliss into the modernist literary circle headed by feminist activist Natalie Clifford Barney. Through her, Bliss met the much-admired Dorothy Richardson. At the age of seventeen, reading Richardson's first volumes of *Pilgrimage*, she had felt in the presence of a kindred soul, and that Richardson was "the only person who [was] writing a real book".[10] In the years to come, Bliss had been her devout friend and loved her deeply.

Although influenced by Richardson's style and feminist ideas, she also sensed in her friend a "curious blind spot", a certain "area of insensitivity to others' needs and feelings" (*Luminous*, xvii). The introduction, by Alexandra Pringle, shed some light on Bliss's life, her work and her friends. My imagination was beginning to fashion a portrait of Eliot as a young girl.

Born in Kingston, Jamaica, in 1903, the daughter of Eva Lees and John Plower Bliss, an English army officer of the West Indian Regiment who was stationed in Jamaica and later in Sierra Leone, Eileen Bliss found herself torn between different cultures. In England, where she was sent with her brother, John (also known as Sonny), to receive a Catholic education,[11] she would spend her holi-

---

10   As quoted in Alexandra Pringle, introduction to *Luminous Isle* by Eliot Bliss (1934; repr., London: Virago Press, 1984), vii. All subsequent references will be made parenthetically in the text.

11   At the age of nine, she was sent by her parents to a boarding convent in Weston-super-Mare, run by French and Irish nuns; the only schools she was sent to were Catholic convents, and the most important of all was the boarding convent in Highgate, where she completed her education.

days with her much-loved grandmother and a circle of "countless, unmarried aunts and uncles", enjoying an "extensive, eccentric family" (*Luminous*, xiv). In Jamaica, she had to endure the rigid, limiting, and, to her, boring code of military behaviour. But in Jamaica, there were also her closest friends, some black, some white, whose home in the mountains became her secret refuge.

From 1923 to 1925 she was back in Jamaica with her brother. Her journey there, and the final decision to leave, are the subject of *Luminous Isle*, together with memories of her Jamaican childhood. Bliss's return to London in 1925 meant severing ties with her family, who later moved to South Africa. A new life was opening up, and she probably felt she had a full range of choices in front of her. Like Emmeline Hibbert in *Luminous Isle*, she thought "she was going towards the future" (302).

In London she consciously cut any, or most, ties with her family, which was still in the colonies. Christened Eileen, she became Eliot. She had luscious, long auburn hair, with golden highlights; she cut it. She had been a faithful follower of the Catholic Church; she left it. She shared an apartment with her best friend from the convent years, the blonde, handsome and talented pianist Susan Curtnoys.[12] Their future together had been carefully planned during their years of education in a Highgate nuns' convent. As she told Alexandra Pringle: "She was a pianist; she was very, very beautiful. In school we always made up our minds we would live together and have a home together"[13] (*Luminous*, xvi). Reading *Luminous Isle*'s introduction, and thinking of *Saraband*'s characters, I could see now how she had woven her autobiography into her writing.

Saraband takes its title from a seventeenth-century dance. Music plays a crucial role in Bliss's writings; here it is a life-giving gift, and the saraband comes to signify the moment of revelation, of recognition and self-awareness.[14]

---

12   Susan Curtnoys, often spelled Courtnoys, would later be the inspiration for the characters of Œnone, Emmeline's friend in *Luminous Isle*, and both Zara and Brenda, Louie's friends in *Saraband*.

13   Later she would move in with nineteen-year-old Patricia Allan-Burns, who became her lifelong companion.

14   What follows is based on articles I previously published: "To Be Sexless, Creedless, Classless, Free: Eliot Bliss: A Creole Writer", *A Goodly Garlande: In onore di Sergio Perosa*. *Annali di Ca' Foscari* 42, no. 4 (2003); and "Islands, Colors and Obsessions: The Other and the Self in Three Creole Writers: Eliot Bliss, Phyllis Shand Allfrey and Jean Rhys", in *Rites of*

The book chronicles the story of Louie, a young girl living, like Eliot, within a large extended family. The arrival of her cousin Timothy, a gifted musician, stimulates her mind. His piano performance would bring what Louie had been waiting for: "He began playing a saraband, soft and slow with a swinging movement accompanied by little trills in the treble. And here she was sitting down and bowing to his authority. She allowed it to him because he had brought with him the long looked-for stimulation of the mind" (*Saraband*, 49).

In *Luminous Isle* (51–52), the role will be taken by Emmeline's friend Œnone ("Life entered through Œnone's finger-tips [. . .]. A world of life and sound [. . .]. Drops of crystal water dripping slowly into a gradually filling pool."

Saraband was welcomed as "a first novel of unusual power".[15] Bliss's prose is clearly influenced by the modernist, and feminist, literary ideas of 1930s London – by Dorothy Richardson's experimental realism, by Virginia Woolf's use of interior monologue – but her style owes more to Henry James and Ford Madox Ford. In her novels, too, things seldom *happen*; all powerful feelings are hidden, though sometimes summoned up in flashbacks. Here, as well, the old world is collapsing; it is actually the same old world, with the same set of worn-out codes, with the same "good people" as protagonists. The events recalled in *Saraband* take place before and around the Second World War, when the world was changing and a new order was taking shape. A new order where women could find their own place, perhaps. Bliss's heroines understand in full the magnitude, the tragedy of what is happening around them. The end of the old world, both in England and in the colonies, is seen and told from their point of view, a woman's point of view, in a society where the pain that tears the soul might be inflicted in the softest tone:

> The end of the world was in the parlour with the stiff-backed chairs. It had been brought to her by the most civilised of people. (*Saraband*, 99)

> She wanted to go. To escape [. . .]. Behind this kind of life from which she had come – the suave, elegant exteriors [. . .], the charming but vacant whole, was a tragedy; small, pitiable, a skeleton hidden in a decently narrow cupboard of the soul. (255)

Passage: Rational/Irrational, Natural/Supernatural, Local/Global, ed. C. Nocera, G. Persico, R. Portale (Soveria Mannelli: Rubbettino, 2003).

15 "Moods", review of *Saraband*, by Eliot Bliss. *Saturday Review of Literature* 8 (1931): 8.

In a review of the 1987 *Saraband* reprint, Robin Bromley described the book as a "wonderfully impressionistic account of a young English girl's struggle to grow up in World War I England",[16] and accordingly, "There is no plot [. . .] there is not much incident. What there is for the reader is a succession of moods, of delicate and lovely emotions: Miss Bliss [. . .] is keenly alive to atmospheres; the country house, the convent, the commercial school, all arouse in her a multitude of sensations. But she does not make the mistake [. . .] of tearing passions to tatters: Her emotions are all recollected in tranquillity."[17]

Indeed, borrowing Conrad's words on the impressionistic writer's task, Bliss's accounts make you see and above all *feel* the inextricable knot of pain and the turmoil of a girl torn by passions she can only vaguely understand and certainly not master yet. Though recounting her own life, Bliss succeeds in keeping her voice outside the narrative and letting Louie's voice emerge with such authentic timbre that it does make you *feel* her emotions as separate from her author's.

Her prose was said to show an "astonishing maturity", and indeed her skill in creating "young women in a state of subdued, but actual rebellion"[18] is remarkable. Just as remarkable is the way she conveys the sense of foreboding without being melodramatic. Both Louie in *Saraband*, and Emmeline (Em) in *Luminous Isle* embark on a journey where they will face difficult yet inevitable choices. As Paul Bailey puts it: "They are remarkable creatures [. . .] because they are not flamboyant, not theatrical, not prominent – as yet – in the battle for the rights of their sex. They are both possessed of loving feelings [. . .]. With the awareness of those feelings is born a set of values – values, Eliot Bliss implies, that may not be so socially acceptable" (*Saraband*, vii–viii).

The two novels are largely autobiographical. They can be read as a whole, covering various periods in Eliot Bliss's life – her education in England, her childhood in Jamaica, the years she spent there before leaving the island forever. Characters seem to float from one novel to the other, almost indistinguishably, chatting and drinking their teas as if the world outside did not exist. They

---

16   Robin Bromley, review of *Saraband*, by Eliot Bliss, *New York Times Book Review*, 3 May 1987, 44.

17   "Moods", 8.

18   Paul Bailey, introduction to *Saraband*, by Eliot Bliss (1931; repr., London: Virago, 1984), vii. All subsequent references will be made parenthetically.

form a big canvas of characters which constitutes a perfect portrait of an era.

But these novels are also more than autobiographical. Their genre may be defined as something between a memoir and a philosophical treatise, an intellectual discourse on *art* and a *feminist* pamphlet on women's possibilities and prospects in the twentieth century. The idea of a feminist perspective runs through both narratives. In a world where one "almost had to have permission to exist if one was a woman" (*Saraband*, 238), where her "talents and gifts" would be "wasted" and "utilized only in their least productive sense" (257), the Bliss heroine's main desire is to be "her own mistress" (52), and in order to do so, she is willing to change her physical appearance, cutting her hair and robbing "herself of a characteristic feature of feminine abandonment" (127).

Bliss's ideas on the woman-artist of the new century, who is capable of offering her own outlook on the interrelation between art, love, feelings and emotions, are expressed by Zara in *Saraband*: "Feeling, you know; emotion. After all, feeling can't be entirely ignored. It's out of feelings that things get made. I think one ought to feel things – as well as do them well [. . .] it's love, not ambition, that makes an artist" (87–89).

Em and Louie are mostly, but not completely, self-portraits. They are said to be "nearly, but not quite, asexual" (*Saraband*, vii). Indeed, far from being asexual, the protagonists of Bliss's works display an elusive sexuality, an inner quality that makes them "exciting and secret, different from all those other people" (*Luminous*, 302). They are girls with passionate hearts and strong feelings whose emotions and passions – banned by social conventions – are never openly expressed.

Consequently, the underlying homosexuality of the characters is never spelled out; it remains unuttered, and the intricate implications of the relationships between Em and her cousin Tim, Em and Zara, Tim and Bernard, are never fully explained.

Indeed, though Tim may be perceived at first as Louie's potential lover, it is clear that their relationship is devoid of physical aspects. It is, rather, a relationship of intellectual fulfilment and communion. Tim is a completion of Louie; to her he is "the height of human achievement", "a work of art", "something marvellous and holy", "the thing she could never be" (*Saraband*, 41).

While *Saraband* is set in England and chronicles Louie's coming-of-age with a diachronic movement – interrupted by epiphanies, and with flashbacks from the Caribbean bursting unexpectedly into the narrative – *Luminous Isle* is set in the Caribbean. It opens with Em as a child (first chapter, "Ambrosia"), and moves on (second chapter, "The Western Path") to Em's return to the island after her school years in England – years that will return in flashbacks as Em ponders her possibilities, her choices, her "destination" (*Luminous*, 50). The prose in *Luminous Isle* is richer, more sensual, and the soft, dreamy stream of consciousness of *Saraband* gives way to a more voluptuous language where Eliot's creole inner self can soar freely.

Passion, which in *Saraband* was "relegated to a place beneath the surface of everyday discourse" (*Saraband*, vi), is conveyed in *Luminous Isle* through the description of natural elements and landscape. While the opening of *Saraband* and its sophisticated description of the smell of winter had a sort of hallucinating, rarefied, dream-like quality, *Luminous Isle* opens with violence and a sense of danger, with the noises and smells of the Caribbean night invading Em's room.

> All along the road from the river the frost made patterns on the ground, and how beautifully the air smelt. [. . .] The sharp air hung over one's head like the blade of a knife. [. . .] Winter had a most exciting smell, it made one think of people whom one knew and yet had never met, places where at some time or other one felt sure one must have lived and yet could not remember. [. . .] The frost hung on the trees, it made them look as if they had gone white during the night from fear . . . smelling the cold air [. . .] the exciting feeling took hold of her, the feeling that at any moment she was going to meet somebody or something. (*Saraband*, 5)

> The North *breeze* was just beginning. At the end of the garden the *mango* tree beside the fence trembled *violently*, and several *over-ripe* mangoes fell to the ground. The air was full of the long shrill humming of the crickets which persisted, never even stopping for a moment, through the otherwise deeply *silent* West Indian night. [. . .] Em listened to the *sinister* zing-zinging all round the house, half terrified, half fascinated, [. . .] she peered into the garden. She would not have been surprised to have seen *evil spirits* standing there in rows. [. . .] The North *breeze* gently stirred the air and blew in, in little puffs – even through the meshes of the mosquito-net with its starchy clean smell – the *smell* of the night. The *smell* of grass, green scented and strong, cut that afternoon, lying in little heaps in the middle of the lawn and already soaked through with night dew; the *smell* of water dripping on to a flower bed from a tap not

quite turned off in the garden, and a faint sweet cold smell from a tree near the bungalow. (*Luminous*, 3–5; emphasis added)

The reader is thrown into a New World, where there is total identification between the natural elements and Emmeline. Each part of the novel, and each phase of Em's life, is marked by violent, relentless natural phenomena (scorching sun, riotous thunderstorms, et cetera) in the background of the indomitable Caribbean landscape.

A thunderstorm and the end of a child's dream closes the first part – "a deep and swift exaltation. Sitting shivering in her white muslin dress with only a white coat on, she felt as if a white fire were whipping the air all around her. [. . .] The dreams of the past were idle hours which had gone for ever" (*Luminous*, 48) – a fiery sun welcomes Em's return to the island in the second. Lying in the deck-chair, she seems to resume the threads of her childhood thoughts: "The past and the future had ceased, and had become merged into the present; as if one were already travelling in eternity. [. . .] travelling towards what? Illusion, perhaps, that one ever travels at all. [. . .] perhaps towards the place one had determined upon long ago" (49).

The protagonist's physical journey from and back to the island is really a journey of self-discovery, where she feels drawn more and more to the island's black population in a way that has no precedent in the colony's white society. Contesting the British "spiritual anaemia of only half-conceived emotions" (*Saraband*, 242), Bliss's women counter with colours and smells of a place she herself cherished and longed for all her life: the Caribbean. "The Blue Mountains one knew as a child. Purple peaks going up into the sky. [. . .] The island lay before one, shaded in green and blue pencil. [. . .] Smells of flowers, lovely mountain smells, heavy-leafed plants fat with rain. How large and near and blue the mountains loomed" (193).

Again and again, I compared the opening pages of *Luminous Isle* to the opening pages of Rhys's *Wide Sargasso Sea*, published more than thirty years later, and found a striking similarity:

Our garden was *large* and *beautiful* as that garden in the Bible – the *tree of life* grew there. But it had gone wild. The paths were overgrown and a smell of dead flowers mixed with the fresh living *smell*. Underneath the tree ferns, tall as forest tree ferns, the *light* was green. *Orchids* flourished out of reach or for some reason *not to be touched*. One was snaky looking, another like an octopus with long thin tentacles bare of leaves hanging from a twisted root. Twice a year the octopus orchid flowered – then not an inch of tentacle showed. It was a bell-shaped mass of white, mauve, deep purples, wonderful to see. The *scent* was very sweet and strong. I never went near it.[19]

The introduction to *Luminous Isle* and Carol Angier's biography made it clear that the two writers were friends, that Rhys knew Eliot's book and that they would often meet in London in the 1950s: "She used to make me delightful West-Indian suppers, and we used to drink an awful lot. Well she could hold it, but it used to make me ill, frequently ill" (*Luminous*, xvii).

The islands, where the battle for freedom is fought – and perhaps also lost – are co-protagonists of these books. The two descriptions might very well come from the same book: the islands, with their dangerous yet irresistible attractions, beautiful and horrific, loom large in both quotes, and, most notably, the colours and the smells – of flowers, dead and alive, of grass, of water, of the night.

If the way these islands are described is similar, so is the relationship between the heroines and their respective islands. Emmeline Hibbert, the protagonist of *Luminous Isle*, thinks that "the bleached hills seemed to run out to meet her with her calm limbo-like brows. [. . .] [T]here was recognition between them and herself. It had not been imagined, it was a feeling, this understanding between herself and the hills" (100).

Antoinette, in *Wide Sargasso Sea*, *is* the island, and the island *is* Antoinette. Rochester (though unnamed in the novel) would do anything to own both, to unveil the secret Antoinette and the island share and hide: "It was a beautiful place – wild, untouched, above all untouched, with an alien, disturbing, secret loveliness. And it kept its secret. I'd find myself thinking, 'What I see is nothing – I want what it *hides* – that is not nothing."[20] The disease of the islands, brought on by parasites, the English colonizers, is described in a similar manner, and it leads the heroines towards a similar disastrous conclusion: exile.

Antoinette, in *Wide Sargasso Sea*, is taken away, deprived even of her name

---

19   Jean Rhys, *Wide Sargasso Sea* (1966; repr., London: Penguin, 1990), 16–17; emphasis added.

20   Ibid., 74.

and identity, by her English husband and forced into exile *and* madness. Emmeline, in *Luminous Isle*, chooses to go into exile of her own free will as a way of keeping her mental sanity. Struck by the impossibility of coming to terms with the "perfect Englishness" of the colony, she sails away, leaving behind her much-loved, golden-coloured island.

The varying sense of place in these novels may also be related to the contrast between reality and dream. Each heroine is torn between the warm Caribbean of her "dream" – a dream that often invades reality and is in turn invaded by it – and cold, alien England.

Emmeline, in *Luminous Isle*, wishes she could "go back to the Island", which is "more real than the people sitting on either side of her" (100), but is driven away by the narrow-mindedness of the "perfect Englishness" of colonial society. To her, "the green-and-gold background of the West Indian home had always been there at the back of all her school days . . . Making her . . . want passionately in the secret depths of her being – almost more than anything else – to go back to the Island" (54).

Why were there no exhaustive studies comparing these two novels?

Although not within the scope of this work, perhaps the time has come for a thorough comparison, an analysis through close textual reading – to shed some light on the influence of *Luminous Isle* on *Wide Sargasso Sea*.

I only knew that Jean Rhys, talking about a possible title for the book, had written Francis Wyndham that she "thought of 'Sargasso Sea' or 'Wide Sargasso Sea' but nobody knew what [she] meant" (29 March 1958).[21] Other than that, at the time I could not find any other reference to the title, or its meaning. Had she also talked to Eliot about it? Since Eliot had written a book on a similar subject, it was to be expected that they would have talked about it, but (at the time) I could not prove it.

❯❯❯❮❮❮

My obsession with the reasons why Eliot Bliss had sunk into oblivion made me neglect all other obligations, mainly writing my paper for the Münster conference. However, Jorge Rademacher, the organizer, was urging me to

---

21 Wyndham and Melly, *Letters of Jean Rhys*, 154.

send an abstract. And so, brought back to reality by his imperative messages – and since actually, at that moment, I had no way of finding any connections between the two West Indian writers – I resolved to complete my paper on "Punctuation in Modernist Fiction: *No More Parades*". Eliot and Jean's mystery would have to wait.

I came back from Münster on 27 June 1999. It was that part of the year when lessons are finished, and I had only a few days to spend in Trieste for exams and office hours before the summer vacation. I was eager to sit at my desk and begin writing to various librarian friends around the world, enquiring about Eliot Bliss. I felt I was embarking on a treasure hunt.

We had not planned to go on vacation that year, but an email that arrived a few days later changed things. Marilyn and Joe Russo, our old friends from New York, with their son Jacob, were coming to Italy from New York for a couple of weeks in August to visit Joe's relatives in Sicily, and were willing to let us stay in their New York apartment. We could take care of their two cats.

Such an opportunity was not likely to come our way again soon, so we gratefully accepted. I *needed* to do more research, needed access to library resources and databases, to rare books collections, to offices and archives, all things that would be impossible from Italy; but I did not have any research funds, so Marilyn's offer was a godsend.

I had met Marilyn and Joe in New York in 1989, while studying for my doctorate. We shared the same corridor on the first floor of 59 East 7th Street, between First and Second Avenue, right across the Caffè della Pace, which served quite decent *cappuccini* and has since been transformed into a trendy restaurant, now called Via Della Pace.

It had been easy to become friends with the Russos: I was from Italy like Joe's parents; we all loved books and had cats – I was then travelling with my own cat, Melissa, my lifelong companion. I was not married at the time, and had no intention to become so.

Now, in 1999, I was a married woman and had a five-year-old son, Alexander.

New York, Bobst Library
17 August–5 September 1999

I travelled with my husband and son, but this time left Melissa behind, not without trepidation, in the hands of a dear friend. She was beginning to age, and the veterinarian had advised us to let her stay home, so we did.

As soon as we decided to take Marilyn up on her offer, I had written Professor Ernest Gilman, at the English department of New York University, asking whether he would be willing to act as my NYU sponsor for the duration of my stay. This would allow me to work once again at Bobst Library, twelve floors of open stacks for me to peruse freely. I had many fond memories of that library and of my friends there, of spending long hours, morning to midnight, reading and scribbling. The beautiful floor is an exact copy of the piazzale in front of the church on the island of San Giorgio, right across from St Mark's Square, in Venice. Looking down from the top floor at Bobst, the sight was breathtaking.[22]

The first thing I did on the first day of my first New York visit, in 1984 – after completing the enrolment procedures for my master's in English literature – was to go to the Bobst Library, and the first person I spoke to was Lynn Palumbo, at the reference desk; she worked there but was also studying for her PhD in Medieval English literature. Years later she would be the maid of honour at my wedding.

In the summer of 1999, upon entering the Bobst Library a day after arriving in New York, I was shocked to discover that George Thompson was no longer there. I had planned to rely on George's memory and capability to help me dig up any long-buried evidence related to Eliot Bliss. As Jim Tuttleton had pointed out, if something was out there, George could find it. George was the best librarian a scholar could hope for, combining a keen love for literature with a detective mind and an encyclopaedic knowledge.

However, I owe a debt of thanks to the librarian who helped me that summer, a young lady whose name I unfortunately do not recall. She sat me

---

22 It is impossible now to look down at it from upper floors. In 2003, two students died by suicide jumping from the ninth or tenth floor, and this led to the installation of tall protective panels along the atrium's railing, to prevent other tragic deaths. Unfortunately, in November 2009, another student died by suicide jumping from the tenth floor.

in front of a computer and taught me how to navigate their newly acquired databases. And right there and then I had my first real break: the Department of Special Collections at McFarlin Library (University of Tulsa) had enriched their "Jean Rhys Collection" with a letter from Eliot Bliss to Jean Rhys.[23]

There was nothing else, but I felt it was important, a key to *something*. That night I emailed the head librarian at McFarlin asking whether, and how, I could read that letter. Not receiving any answer during my stay in New York, I decided I would try again upon my return to Italy.

In the meantime, the young librarian found an old volume of *Who Was Who among English and European Authors: 1931–1949*. The awfully brief entry under Eliot Bliss included only her date of birth, 1903, and the name of one of the convents where she had received her Catholic education, but, to my surprise, the list of her published works included a third novel, *The Albatross*, published by Cobden-Sanderson, which was not mentioned anywhere else, with a publication date, 1935.

So, in the summer of 1999, what I had regarding Eliot's critical bibliography consisted of a single chapter in O'Callaghan's book,[24] where she was considered in a group with Jean Rhys and Phyllis Shand Allfrey but was not examined individually; the 1980s introductions to the reprints of her two known books, *Saraband* (1931) and *Luminous Isle* (1934); a couple of reviews of her two books, written at the time of publication, which I could read on microfilm at Bobst Library; and a few footnotes and letters in books about other authors.

It was not until 2001, during a university break, that I had time to look again at the University of Tulsa website and discover that McFarlin had in its possession not only additional letters from Eliot to Rhys, but also her diaries: nineteen volumes for the years 1959 and 1963–1980.

---

23   Today the collection has been enriched by more of Eliot Bliss's material – letters, photos, mementos and a lock of her hair.

24   Since then other works have dealt with Eliot Bliss's work, such as Omise'ke Natasha Tinsley, *Thiefing Sugar: Eroticism between Women in Caribbean Literature* (Durham, NC: Duke University Press, 2010).

CHAPTER 2

>>>«««

The Diaries

Venice
2 October 2001

From: Michela A. Calderaro
To: Lori Curtis
Subject: McFarlin Library and Eliot Bliss
Date: 2 October 2001

Dear Ms. Curtis,[1]

I teach English and Post-Colonial Literature at the University of Trieste (Italy).

I'm currently working on a critical study of *Luminous Isle* by Creole writer Eliot (Eileen) Bliss and am encountering incredible difficulties in finding information about her. I heard she died not long ago, but this can be just a rumour, since in your catalogue of special collections only her date of birth is quoted.

If she is still alive, I was wondering if you could help me find out whether she would be willing to talk to me.

Also, since I live in Italy it is quite impossible for me to travel to Tulsa and do my research there. Could you please let me know whether there is any possibility of reading her diaries or letters through an interlibrary loan or by other means?

I will appreciate enormously your assistance.

Regards,

Michela A. Calderaro

---

1 Lori Curtis is not at McFarlin anymore, but we are still in touch, and I still enjoy her friendship; she gave me permission to reproduce our email exchange.

From: Lori Curtis
To: Michela A. Calderaro
Subject: Re: McFarlin Library and Eliot Bliss
Date: 31 October 2001

Dear Professor Calderaro,

I must first apologize for the delay in responding to your query. Somehow I missed seeing the email and just found it today.

I'm afraid I don't have much information at all about Eliot Bliss. In fact, there doesn't seem to be much known about her at all. When we were offered the letters from Jean Rhys to Bliss in 1994, Bliss was already deceased but it was not known the exact date.

At one time she had shared a house with a Mrs Patricia Allan Burns of 152 Plaw Hatch Close, Bishop's Stortford, Hertfordshire CM23 5BJ, ENGLAND. Mrs Burns is the one who had the letters and diaries to sell. However, at that time she was quite elderly and ill herself and I fear she may have passed away herself. But I would definitely write to the address to see if she is still living and if she can offer you any information.

Regarding access to Eliot Bliss's diaries and correspondence, it is our policy to require written permission from the author or the estate prior to providing scholars with photocopies of such material, as it is not known who may hold the copyright to the Bliss material. Virago publishers reissued her SARABAND and LUMINOUS ISLE awhile back; I would suggest checking with them to see if they know who holds the copyright for Bliss material.

Eliot Bliss's The Diaries however pose a problem. First, we would ask that you make an attempt to track down who holds the copyright to Bliss's manuscripts, etc. Again, I would write to Mrs Burns and to Virago Press to see if they have any information. In cases where it is not possible to locate an heir, estate, or other individual to whom copyright was assigned, we waive the requirement with proof that an attempt was made.

Tulsa Studies in Women's Literature, which is published here at the University of Tulsa, offers grants to individuals to travel to Tulsa to make use of the collections. I'm not sure of the amount of each grant, but I would highly recommend writing to inquire. Such a grant could permit you to come to Tulsa during a break at the University of Trieste or during the summer holiday to work with the material here. The grants have proven very useful to other scholars who have had to travel from such distances as South Africa to use the collections. I would certainly check into it. The address to which you should write is Linda Frazier [. . .]

Shall I fax the forms that we would need to have you complete, or would you prefer that I drop them in the mail to you?

Again, I do sincerely apologize for the lengthy delay in responding to your query. I don't know how I missed seeing your email, but am glad I did find it and hope that we can find a way to solve the problem of access to the Eliot Bliss diaries.

Sincerely,

Lori N. Curtis

Head of Special Collections

From: Michela A. Calderaro

To: Lori Curtis

Subject: Re: McFarlin Library and Eliot Bliss

Date: 18 February 2002

Dear Ms Curtis,

Following your suggestion I did write (twice) to Ms Burns and Virago Press regarding the copyright to Eliot Bliss's material. Unfortunately, no one answered.

If you wish I could fax you my copies of such letters to prove that I tried to get their permission.

I am also faxing you the forms you sent me back in November 2001 along with a brief description of the subject and purpose of my research.

Of course I vow to fulfil the "Policies and Regulations Governing the Use of Manuscripts and Archival Collections".

In a few days I will also mail my application for a Travel-to-Collection Grant, as you kindly suggested. And I hope this will allow me to study at McFarlin and work with Eliot Bliss's Diaries.

Thanks again for your assistance and kindness.

Sincerely,

Michela A. Calderaro

≫≪

Tulsa Studies in Women's Literature awarded me a travel-to-collection grant to do my research at McFarlin Library, and in July 2003 the deciphering of Eliot Bliss's diaries began – as did a search that continues to this day.

Before travelling to Tulsa, however, I wanted to try to find out more about *The Albatross*.

In 1999, after coming back from New York, I had begun inquiring about Cobden-Sanderson, the book's registered publisher, only to discover it was no longer active. I did some research, together with the librarians at the University of Trieste, trying to find out to whom they had left their archives. We couldn't find anything, and so I let it rest for the time being.

Now that I had some free time before travelling, I tried again.

The best source of information regarding anything to do with books used to be "The Book People List", a mailing list of book lovers – librarians, experts, scholars. I had been a member for quite a while, and enjoyed the vast knowledge and love for books shared by other members, especially the list moderator, the invaluable John Mark Ockerbloom. Sadly, the list had closed in 2007, ten years after its creation.

I posted an enquiry regarding both her publishers, Cobden-Sanderson and Peter Davies, and many members tried to help.

I was told that Cobden-Sanderson were publishers of poetry, that they had begun as fine bookbinders, and was given a link where I might be able to find some information (http://www.fiveroses.org/Letterpress.htm).

The last books they published dated 1939 (only 6 items, compared with 45 for 1938). Probably, but it is only my speculation, they could not survive the outbreak of war.

On the British Library Public Catalogue, one can find several books published by them in the early 1980s but only in association with a publisher called Heinemann – the link for this publisher was also provided (http://www.heinemann.co.uk).

As for Peter Davies, the suggestion was to have a look at http://www.greenhill books.com/gbn/115/life_cycle_publishing.html.

Unfortunately, none of the links led me anywhere.

My husband and I decided to travel to New York first, where I could conduct some research at Bobst, and then fly to Oklahoma, for what I felt was going to be a great adventure.

Tulsa
6–24 July 2003

We were warmly welcomed by Linda Frazier and the staff of Tulsa Studies, as well as the personnel at McFarlin. I shared my project information and received their enthusiastic support. I would work at the library from nine o'clock in the morning to one in the afternoon, take a short break for lunch, and then back to work until five, when, according to the summer schedule, the library would close.

It was not a bad arrangement after all. At five o'clock I would join my husband and my son, Alexander, whom I had dragged to Tulsa, for a swim in the campus pool.

The room in the library, where I was set up, was dim and cold. There was a lamp on the table where the rare papers rested. The air conditioner was going full blast. The precious documents at the Rare Book Room need to be protected, and the temperature is always adjusted for their benefit. Scholars have to make do (even those who hate air conditioners). I would put on a heavy sweater and wear sneakers, so my feet would not freeze. I was sharing the space with a kind librarian, who would never leave the room while I was there. We both froze.

I could examine one box at a time. I had nineteen diaries to read, but I felt confident: I've always been a fast reader; it could be done.

I had in front of me Eliot Bliss's memories. I could begin to unravel her mysteries.

Box 1, Folder 1: 1959–1960

Upon opening the 1959 diary, my heart sank. Bliss's handwriting was incomprehensible. I suddenly felt I could never succeed in reading a single page, forget the whole seven-thousand-page collection. I asked Lori Curtis and Milissa Burkart, the Special Collections librarians, if they could help decipher a couple of pages, thinking I could then go on by myself. Milissa had taken a course in deciphering handwriting, especially European.

We succeeded in decoding a few words, only to discover that Eliot would not always write words in the same way. Little by little, however, I began to make sense of a few words per page.

She seemed to have been always quite ill and in terrible physical pain.

The first page of the 1959 Royal Collins diary (three-day) carried this handwritten inscription: "Eliot Bliss, Firlands, Bishop's Stortford 1959 Also 1960" (Firlands being an area in the town of Bishop's Stortford, Hertfordshire). The following page carried another handwritten inscription: "End Pages of 1958 Diary used to January 4th Sunday". The 1959 diary was then written throughout. Inside there were also dozens of densely written loose pages, covering the entire year of 1960, many with no clear date on them.

On the last of the loose pages, dated Saturday, 31 December, she writes: "End of [incomprehensible word] year on this improvised Diary. [. . .] a bad year." "Cold", "bitterly cold", "sadness", "loneliness", "isolation" and "depression" are the words that recur most throughout the nineteen diaries, and that set the tone of my journey into the recorded life of Eliot Bliss.

Distressed about my difficulties deciphering her handwriting, I briefly glanced through the other diaries, hoping to find some clues.

While I was trying to figure out a way to pull Eliot Bliss out of oblivion and make her better known to the public, I began wondering about the ethics of scholarly research, questioning my own reading of her diaries. Were they intended to be read by someone else, or would she resent my prying into her privacy? I smiled to myself when I got to the end of her 1971 diary. There she wrote:

> Notes on My Diaries
> (Years:
> (For whoever may read them, or try to – after my departure to "The Other World")
> Signs at the bottom of each page were made [unintelligible word] for my own wish to record – mostly physical things.

This was followed by a list of acronyms, explanations and medication brand names. On the days she worked, she would write the letter "W" on the right hand side of the page, or the letter "W" with a little crown on top when she would "work on a play *Seti*". "NW" would mean "No work done", "LW" for "A little work". There was also a list of people's names:

People mentioned in Diaries

S – Sylvia (an old friend)

P – Pat (my friend)

C – a House-Help we had for 5 years (Connie P . . .?)

Miss S – another H.H – a young woman (. . .?)

JK – John Kirkwood – an old friend of Sylvia's who became a friend of mine who I liked

John – John Williams – a great friend for [?] many years who I meet and . . . very fond of.

B – Brian Pilcher – a taxi driver – (and friend) who has driven me since 1965

SD – Sonny [?] [brother] (who died [now dead?] – 1967) and Dot his wife[2]

Cairn – a much loved friend American (died 1965)

Anna – Anna Wickham a great friend and poet (killed herself 1947) who is [?] often in my thoughts also dreams

Jim – Jim Hepburn her eldest son – who[3] I've known for many years –

George – his brother, Anna's youngest son –

George B – George Burton, an old friend[,] son of my old and loved doctor

Miss S – Miss Smith. House-help

BH – The Boar's Head Hill [?] Windhill BS

She had envisioned that someday someone would find her diaries and "try" to read them, fully aware that it would pose deciphering problems. Unfortunately, in the diaries she mentioned many other people whose names proved impossible to identify.

With the little note as my guide, I went back to the earlier diaries, and felt more confident that I would be able to establish the network of her friends and relationships, or at least part of it.

Many times I ran across Jean Rhys's name, either in the form of little notes written in the corners of pages, such as "letter to Jean Rhys" or "letter from Jean Rhys", or within the long entries, which were, again, impossible to figure out. So I decided to look into the Jean Rhys Collection, where I hoped to find some clues.

Again, I was warned that no photocopying of the Jean Rhys material was allowed, since I did not have permission from the Jean Rhys Estate in the person

---

2 Eliot's brother, Sonny, and his wife, Dot, had two daughters, Sally and Sue.

3 As mentioned elsewhere, I have tried, where possible, to retain Eliot Bliss's spelling, grammar and syntax.

of the copyright holder, Mrs Moerman, to whom I had written the year before.

There it was, however: the reference to *Wide Sargasso Sea* that I had been looking for.

In one of her unpublished letters to Bliss, dated 16 March 1959, which I could read (but cannot quote here), Rhys thanked the lesser-known writer for sharing her knowledge of what the "Sargasso Sea" was and acknowledged Bliss was the first to have understood the meaning of those words. What had Eliot written? What had she shared with Jean?

As of today, some of Eliot Bliss's letters to Jean Rhys cannot be read, as we have not yet been granted access by Mrs Moerman. Nevertheless, back then, in the freezing-cold room at McFarlin's, I felt rewarded. I now knew for sure that between February and March 1959, the two writers had discussed the meaning of the Sargasso Sea.[4]

At the time of this correspondence, Rhys was in Cornwall in a place so "cold that freezes your heart and marrow" (letter to Selma Vas Diaz, 5 February 1959).[5] She was struggling to write her masterpiece, plagued by the flu and caring for her sick husband; at the same time, Bliss was in Hertfordshire, also struggling with poor health and financial difficulties. In one of her letters, Rhys mentioned that she was keeping all of Bliss's "cards", and jokingly added that she was going to frame them all once she would become rich.

⟫⟩⟪⟨

I would take short breaks from decoding in order to rest my eyes. I was beginning to realize that a complete transcription of her diaries was beyond human capability, but was trying to follow the web of connections she had established. It was clear from the notes at the bottom of each diary page that she would write quite a number of letters a day, and that she had actually corresponded with most influential writers of the twentieth century. But besides her letters to Jean Rhys, I could not trace any other correspondence.

---

4   Unpublished correspondence between Eliot Bliss and Jean Rhys here and below is courtesy of the Department of Special Collections, McFarlin Library, University of Tulsa (Tulsa, Oklahoma). Consulting the correspondence and "The Eliot Bliss Diaries" was made possible thanks to a *Tulsa Studies in Women's Literature* Travel-to-Collection Grant.

5   Wyndham and Melly, *Letters of Jean Rhys*, 160.

Just then Lori Curtis came to my rescue, suggesting we might in fact trace some of Eliot's letters in the Horace Gregory Collection, located at Syracuse University Library, Department of Special Collections.

Upon my return to Italy, I got in touch with the head librarian at Syracuse, and I was then able to read part of the correspondence between Horace Gregory and Eliot Bliss. I finally understood how Eliot had met Jean Rhys. It had begun with Dorothy Richardson, who introduced her to Horace Gregory,[6] who in turn sent a letter to Jean Rhys introducing the young fellow-Caribbean writer.

But regarding other issues, I was at a loss.

Who was Sylvia?

BOX 1, FOLDER 1: 1959–1960

As she stated in her notes, the initial *S* stood for Sylvia, "(an old friend)" and *P* for Pat "(my friend)". According to entries in the diaries, this person, Sylvia, had been living with them since 1955. Her full name was not mentioned. How did she get there, why, and for how long? But mainly, *who* was she?

Now and then a few typed pages provided relief for my eyes: those and various loose notes and letters shed light on the relationship among the three women – or at least, this is what I thought at the time.

Within the pages of the 1959–1960 diaries lay a letter from George Hepburn, dated "Brighton 17 May 1959", addressed to Bliss at the Royal Hotel, Woburn Place. Sylvia appears to have gone away.

> My Dear Eliot,
> Thank you for your letter – and for the invitations [. . .].
> I hope you enjoy your stay in London – the theatres etc., and hope Sylvia is sufficiently recovered to come and meet you. I wonder still, whether she will ever return to you in B. Stortford.

The phrase "return to you" seemed to me to indicate some sort of an intimate relationship. Were they lovers? And what did Patricia think of this new presence in their lives?

---

6   Eliot Bliss, letter to Horace Gregory, 15 September 1936 (Horace Gregory Collection, courtesy of Syracuse University Library, Special Collections, Syracuse University [Syracuse, New York]).

I found no entries for the following week, from 26 to 31 May, when Eliot was probably in London. But for the period just before it and immediately after, I found references to a correspondence with Sylvia. By July she was not back, and on 18 July, Bliss writes: "Patricia wrote a letter to S. for me. Felt v. depressed".

Brief entries, such as "wrote letter to S.", are to be found through October 1959, when Sylvia came back for what seems to have been a brief visit, then again through most of 1960.

Tuesday, May 31st

Hot day but cool evening frosts both nights. Letters from S with £3 in p.o.'s Mrs Levy did not come. I waited for her, had smll [sic] brandy, not feeling well. Pain in hands in morning. After tea I tried typewrite and was right about it I can type, but keys stiff & some sticking, cannot do much on it but started letter to S. Worked on "R. from the Wilderness" nearing end.

Wednesday, June 1st

After night frost an intensely hot day, went up to 80 and extreme humidity. Woke in pain Took s. s. Got up 11. I rang Mrs Leyden at 11.15. Mrs L. sick she says but coming on Friday. I only hope this latter is true. Told Mrs Leyden how I am. She was sorry but doubt if she took it in. Asked Bennet [a small department store] to send things but they were uncertain as opening new shop. (They didn't either) Finished letter to S. but no one to post it. Rang Barkiers [? crossed over letters] re trolley. Too dear. Felt very done up with health and legs bad from it. Also very depressed. Get terribly tired when no one comes also neurotic. Have been too much alone during the past awful year. Worked in eveing [sic] on end of "R. from the Wilderness" last lines need re-writing. Felt dreadful fatigue feeling which usually preceedes [sic] an attack. Meant to write Times book Club re Writers & Artists Year Book and Laurence Durrell's Collected poems. Went bed early very depressed and di [sic] not go to sleep till 2.20 and woke at 7. It was hot. Wrote this up Thursday.

Whit-Monday, June 6th

Cloudy day with rain about. Temperature dropping steadily from 74 to the sixties. Got up 11.30. P not in good temper as she slept badly and has her curse and was like this all day. Did not have lunch till 25 to 4 as she was ironing then said it was my fault! As usual her bad mood re-acted on me and I got bad tempered but said little. Most weekends are like this anyway now and it takes me some time to recover after. Went bed 4.45 to 6.15. Did not have tea till nearly 7. After tea P. mended and sewed her underclothes etc. I did my desk and cleared a space on it but it hurt both hands and legs to do it and felt terrible feeling of exhaustion and vertigo afterwards. anyway cant type at it as cant get up or pull out the chair in my present state without causing pain. I typed short note to Sylvia re trains. After supper and after 10 Barbara rang up – and P answered phone and rather told her off this time. Went bed 10.30 very tired, much cooler, felt very depressed. wrote this up next day in sitting room. No work done (5th day) Bian slept under my bed. She came in about 1 o'clock

Bian, I was to find out, was one of the numerous cats that kept Eliot company throughout her life; another one would be Bimbo.

Who was Barbara? A friend? A "house help"? Another lover? It seemed Patricia did not like her. Why? Perhaps I had overlooked references to her and other people while focusing my search on Sylvia.

The handwriting got more difficult to interpret, probably because of the pain caused by her arthritis. From a few clear words I could understand that she was working on a poem, "Blowing Up in Rain", that on 7 June she received two letters from Sylvia, and that on 8 June "P made S's bed for her in sitting room," and she also got "a bottle of wine for me. Shall have a drink tomorrow". It was clear that Patricia and Eliot were expecting Sylvia to be back soon.

Finally, on 10 June she writes: "Got up early expecting Sylvia who did not come till 3.15 – on last train [. . .] S. in a bit of a state [. . .] S talking a lot – has a bad cough and her ankles swell. [. . .] Looks ill. The cats remember her. P came back late."

The life in the household goes on as before. Sylvia is described as looking very ill, having had a heart attack, and therefore she is no help in the house. Patricia runs all the errands and takes care of the house, though they had a "house help":

Saturday, June 11th
"P. did shopping and lunch"

Sunday, June 12th
"P did my bed for me"

Saturday, September 18th
in day P did the hall, sitting room and kitchen, and beat the mats. Put blue

mat down in hearth. After tea not feeling at all good and fearful tiredness also bad indigestion. Went to bed for rest of evening. No work, could not concentrate. Read. Did exercises. P quite pleasant. Put the West Indian basket of my Mother's in sitting room. My right hand too bad to write this up so typed it on Monday evening.

It appears that Sylvia actually went away again, but that by October she was back in Bishop's Stortford. From a typed loose note:

Saturday, October 22nd
    Poured with rain most of the day. I slept a bit better tho woken once by S. P went to work in mroning [sic] and returned in very bad temper and dreadful atmosphere for rest of day. She not speaking to S. or much to me. S went out to Bennets and for cigs and bought ham and some cheese. I got the lunch 3.15 after P had gone and S had a heraty [hearty] meal. Has the appetite of a workman. I washed up felt v tired and went bed and slept for a little. After tea I re-read Part I. 1–23 not as bad as I thought No typing done. Difficult to work in this dreadful atmosphere with P like this. and S. being tiresome. She is however getting better physically. P said at night she did not see how S was going to live on her own, can manage less than usual and it would not be safe. She cant stay here either. Late at night I found centipede on my bed to my horror, was reading [a]nd managed to stop it from coming further up. Got it onto the floor but when I got out to kill it, it had vanished. I loathe these things. How had it got on bed in first place? They drop from ceilings. I killed one I think in the spring of 1959. Weather turned very mild, and it was a mild night. Dreadful day from weather point of view and atmosphere in house.

The place was always chilly, and Eliot suffered from lack of sleep, resorting to chloral to get some rest. Life was not easy, and the atmosphere in the house was getting very tense.

Sylvia stayed, notwithstanding the tension. The humidity and the cold were certainly detrimental to her shaky health. She would get money from a friend, John Kirkwood (diary entry, Thursday, 17 November 1960) and occasionally gave Eliot some pounds back – she owed Eliot some.

There was also a mention of a "Peggy" in relation to Sylvia, and I could later identify her as Peggy Kirkaldy, a friend of Eliot, Jean Rhys and Dorothy Richardson. On the same pages she would also mention a "Betty", whom I could identify later as Betty Fleishoff, a dear friend going back to her days in Jamaica.

Some additional typewritten pages provided more evidence of the rising conflicts among the three women:

Saturday, November 26th

she [Patricia] had forgotten to get S her cigarettes and had to go out again and stayed out over an hour to get out of the place. Did not put up my type-writer and I could do no work. Did a little reading over of . . . but felt worried and angry with S. Also with P. She really is in a state. Drink, sup, and we went to bed late. And I did not sleep till 3 a.m. and had to take more chloral which does not suit me. Got warmer at night.

By the end of 1960, Sylvia was away again; at this point I wondered whether she had to be hospitalized.

⋙⋘

Throughout the early 1960s Eliot would work extensively on various poems, novels and plays – some new, some old, which she would edit. On 15 March 1963, she wrote she had resumed working on a novel she had written between 1951 and 1955, *Passion in Dullmouth*, which she would also revise in 1967; and on 8 March 1963 she wrote she had finished correcting *Return from the Wilderness*, though she would edit it again and again during the summer and also in the following years. She would also revise "My Favourite Goddess", an essay, something she had already been working on back in 1955. Often she would work on a piece she called "S.S.", without ever mentioning the full title, unless, but I cannot prove it, the acronym stood for "Short Story". The list of titles poems, plays, novels is impressive, and so is the time she devoted to revising and correcting them, especially considering that she was constantly ill; most of the daily entries would begin with the same words: "woke in pain".

Occasionally she would take short trips to London, often staying at the County Hotel (Upper Woburn Place, wc1) but sometimes enjoying the hospitality of the Hepburn family.

The 1963 diary, just like all the others, proved impossible to decipher, except for a few entries, now and then, that helped me somewhat grasp the household atmosphere shared by the three women – though not, at that moment, the true nature of their relationship.

On 17 September she wrote: "Slept 1–7 woke in pain. P. made me coffee [. . .] S. annoyed me at breakfast and I lost my temper – but I was very much provoked! After that she was silent I regretted it."

BOX 1, FOLDER 3: 1964

Nineteen sixty-four seemed to have been an extremely productive year: she was revising previous works, such as "Secret Journal", which she had written in the 1940s, but also beginning new short stories: "The Borderland", "On the Lot", "Dante", "The Affair". The correspondence with Jean Rhys was constant.

In December they began packing their belongings before moving out of Firlands. John Kirkwood helped them, and Eliot's leg was in pain. There are a few entries like "C. and I packed" [C. being Connie, the household help], "P. and I alone", "P and I had a row". Sylvia was not with them in those days, but she joined them again soon after the move. Then on 8 December: "We left Firlands after 16 years."

BOX 1, FOLDER 4: 1965

As with all the other diaries, I had to resort to the loose notes and paper clippings to get an idea of what her life was like, what she was writing and what she was going through. One of the notes referred to the play, *Seti*:

1391–1917 approx date of
. . . of Seti I
Seti died 1304
Tutankhamen 1361–69
[. . .]
Seti's father
. . . in the day of Horemhah
Paramesses took the name of
Ramsesses the 1st with his
Reign began the 19th Dynasty[7]

---

7 Dates and spelling of names do not coincide with some history books. It should be

A clipping from a local newspaper advertised a "Reward offered for return or an accurate information concerning much loved large ginger and white Tom Cat (formerly of Firlands). Missing since January 30 from 152 Plaw Hatch Close, Bishop's Stortford. Answers to name of 'Tarti' or 'Ginger'. Right eye missing. Well marked, white paws, good teeth. Nine years old. – Tel. between 11 a.m. and 4 p.m. or after 6 p.m. Bishop's Stortford 51766."

Cats were indeed part of Eliot's life. They kept her company when she felt lonely or was depressed.

Ever more frustrated by Bliss's handwriting, and trying to get the gist of her life, I concentrated on the notes written in the corners of each page. At the bottom she would write how much work she did that day, which kind of pills or medications she took, how many drinks (and there were a lot) she consumed and whom she wrote to; in the left upper corner she would describe, often in parenthesis, the weather and mark certain important events.

In the left upper corner of the page dated 24 May, she scribbled: "(Fine and [warm] day)" and immediately below "(Cairn died in U.S.)", then again at bottom right: "(Cairn died)". On that page she wrote more elaborately about her friend's death: "At 2.45 a telegram arrived (a cable from U.S.) from Cairn's mother saying she had died that morning and may be buried on [. . .] in Washington. A dreadful shock. Told S. Then sat down to think what I should do [. . .] (Cairn was 58 or 9, we had known each other for 32 years)." Another inscription in the upper left corner of 26 May read: "(Cairn cremated in Washington"). During the following days she would repeatedly mention Cairn: "thought a great deal about Cairn", "When Cairn came."

In yet another loose note she wrote more about Cairn's death, and her feelings about it. Unfortunately, there were only a few sentences: "I had another fit of depression late tonight. Rather like the [incomprehensible words] Cairn died" and then, "Don't want to drop down dead have not made my will yet!"

On 31 December, she closed the diary saying: "Very glad to see this thoroughly bad year out. '5' in years are unlucky numbers in my life always."

---

noted, however, that dates related to Ancient Egypt are often controversial, since various historians date certain events differently, and spelling varies according to the Western language one uses.

The diary's last page lists what must have been significant dates, and again she wrote "24 May Cairn died".

Who was Cairn?

⟫⟪

In 1966 she finished *Seti*, and on 29 October posted a note:

> At the Court of Seti
> A dedication to play
> For Seti
> 'Beloved of Ptah'
> Who brought me peace
> from the Ancient World

As she would do with her other diaries, on the last page she summarized the main events of the year, and though saying "I finished my play Seti on Feb. 4th", she continued to revise it well into the late 1960s.

All women in the house fell ill at some time or another: Eliot, who had to go to the hospital for her knee; Patricia; Sylvia, who fell and broke her ankle; and even Connie, the house help. This too is defined as "another bad year", and as a last blow she also lost the little pension she had been receiving for some time: "last part of my RLF [Royal Literary Fund] Pension which I had for 10 years (1957). This is a blow." However, from some other scribbled notes in the left corner of some pages (for instance, 15 July) it seems that the Royal Literary Fund sent her letters "with cheque", so probably somebody decided to ease her financial situation.

She was constantly thinking about death: "(Had my death foretold in a dream)."

In 1967 she wrote short stories ("The Novelist's Daughter", "Associations", "Conversations in the Kitchen", "The Essence", "The Dream", "Director of Souls"), and revised novels she had written in the past (*Hostile Country*, written in 1930–1946, and *Passion in Dullworth,* which she had begun in 1952, then revised in 1955, 1958 and also in 1963). Starting from the mid-1960s she was more and more interested in the supernatural and focused on ESP (extrasensory perception).

The year 1968 was one of intensive work, or rather re-work. Beside new and old poems, she often mentioned working on short stories and plays, "The Dispossessed", "Dante", "Speech with a Stranger", she even revised *Luminous Isle*, *Seti*, and *Return from the Wilderness*.

Her interest in ESP intensified, and after finding a copy of her own "Vision" (written in 1963), she started revising it, and also began working on "The Other World", Part I and Part II.

By 1969 things began to really go bad. She injured her hips, and on 9 September entered hospital – to be released only after ten blood transfusions and eight long weeks. Convalescence was not easy, and she needed what she called "sticks" in order to walk. Also, her hands hurt, and she had difficulties writing; cortisone caused swelling and did not alleviate the pain.

Among the pages, I found two envelopes, one postmarked 13 June 1969, the other 27 November 1969, addressed to a certain Mrs Gough, 152 Plaw Hatch Close – same address as Eliot's – and in Eliot's handwriting. I went back to the month of June to check whether I had missed any mention of Mrs Gough. It was extremely difficult to discern what was important and what was not – Eliot's handwriting made everything look like a long scribble, a list of unintelligible words and letters. She was home during that week, and was also home around 27 November.

Was Mrs Gough another lover? A friend lodging with them?

My frustration was growing, and I felt like giving up. I had only a couple of weeks to solve the mystery of Eliot Bliss's disappearance. The answer was in front of my eyes: poverty, illness, isolation in a "hostile country", no contact with what she still thought of as "her world", London, her literary circles, her friends. At least she still had the friendship and warmth of the Hepburn family – as testified by her many loose notes and correspondence.

Back to 1969. She left hospital on 1 November:

> Left hospital. 3.30 – after 8 weeks and three days –
> walked out [. . .]
> Last of the fine weather
> Very weak shaky
> B. drove us home.
> S. Stayed up to see me. Looks
> ghastly or ill. I was shocked
> at her appearance.

"B.", as I recalled from Eliot's list of names, was Brian Pilcher, a driver and a friend.

Indeed Sylvia was not well, and two days later she would fall badly and need hospitalization. Her situation appeared serious right away. On 3 November, Eliot would write: "Sylvia had [a] fall in her room. 11.30 pm–12, called ambulance and she went into hospital with broken femur – the 2nd time x other leg".

She would never leave the hospital.

Throughout December, Eliot was very sick. Her joints would always be swollen and painful, and she fell once again into deep depression. Because of her condition, she was unable to go and visit Sylvia in the hospital, so it fell to Patricia to do so. The news she would bring back was not at all what Eliot wished to hear.

John Kirkwood would often visit both Sylvia and Eliot, and his visits would always lift Eliot's spirit.

The day before Christmas, on what would be Patricia's last visit with her, Sylvia asked about Eliot and the cats.

Sylvia died at one thirty in the morning on Christmas Day.

After her friend's death, not a single day passed without Eliot thinking of Sylvia, and missing her deeply. John Kirkwood, John Williams and Jim Hepburn surrounded Eliot with their affection and arranged Sylvia's cremation; John Kirkwood had an obituary published in the papers, with the date of the funeral: "GOUGH On Dec. 26, 1969, in hospital at Bishop's Stortford. SYLVIA, formerly wife of the late WILFRED HUGH JULIAN GOUGH, Welsh Guards, in her 77th year. Funeral at Parndon Crematorium, Harlow, Essex, at 2.30 p.m. on Friday, Jan. 2, 1970. Flowers may be sent to Samuel Robinson, The Causeway, Bishop's Stortford, Herts" (*Daily Telegraph*, 30 December 1969[8]).

So Mrs Gough was Sylvia.

On 31 December, the blow of Sylvia's death was to be aggravated by a phone call from George Gough, her son: "He has seen the notice and will come for funeral [incomprehensible words] and mad [. . .]. with everything. I felt this would happen. Felt ill."

---

8   Later, on 24 December 1971, Eliot put the following "in memoriam" in the *Daily Telegraph*: "GOUGH SYLVIA Dec. 26, 1969, at Bishop's Stortford. A wise and witty and charming woman. A much loved deeply missed friend. Eliot and Pat."

She became more and more ill and depressed as the day of the funeral approached: "Felt ill . . . nausea and loneliness over Sylvia's death. Alone all day. Dark" (1 January 1970). Even the cats, especially Bimbo, were "restless" and looking around for Sylvia.

The presence of George Gough seemed to preoccupy Eliot a great deal.

The new year opened in darkness and sadness, and with the realization that the future would just be gloomier.

> Thursday, 1st January
> Dark, cold and miserable day.
> [. . .]
> Missed Sylvia in the house.
> [. . .]
> Sylvia with us 14 years, except for parts of 1959–60 when she was at [. . .] for a bit and in May 1961 when she broke her arm in London and I sent a car for her. [. . .]
> She was 63 when I met her in London in 1955 in the Fitzroy and asked her down here, and [. . .] her 77th year.

A "happy birthday" card between the pages of the diary indicated Sylvia's birthday as 28 April, but her memorial card said she was born on 1 April.[9]

The funeral took place on 2 January. George Gough rang up early in the morning. He had stayed overnight at some inn, he had a car, and would meet them at the crematorium in Harlow. Eliot would not go; Patricia went with John Williams and John Kirkwood. They came back around 3:15 p.m., with George Gough, and they all had tea.

Eliot describes him as being a "nervous and peculiar" man, and she herself, throughout the day, as feeling "ghastly and tired".

> John Williams and Gough and we had tea. I felt ghastly and tired. GG looked at Sylvia's things. man peculiar and nervous. He left and JK left at 10 to 5. John before and I went to bed slept a bit [. . .]. Very sad day and P feeling ghastly. I miss Sylvia very much – tho' one knew it was coming. we did not expect it now. She had [. . .] nice flowers[10] over the coffin in chapel [. . .] am very exhausted.

---

9   Copy of the writing in the Book of Remembrance at Harlow Crematorium.
10   The "List of Floral Tributes" made by Daniel Robinson and Sons, Funeral Directors, carried the following names: George [George Burton], Eliot and Pat, John Keith Stubbs

The scene must have been surreal: a small house in the country, a group of civilized and well-mannered people, related to each other through a dead woman, having tea – an apparently calm and quiet assembly, surrounded by a certain melancholy. Yet certain words found here and there in the diary pages paint a totally different picture.

I could not pinpoint an exact phrase, but my impression was that Eliot feared the presence of George Gough and that he was uncomfortable being there.

At the end of the 1970 diary, she made a list of names and addresses: the first is George Gough, followed by the address of a club in London.

⟫⟪

Later in January she resumed focusing on her poems and short stories, then in May began working on "Sylvia. A Memory". Every day she would write how much she missed Sylvia, "dreadfully", as if life had become suddenly empty.

The depressive mood that had characterized the diaries intensified, if possible, after Sylvia's death; it was clear, at least to me, that Sylvia, though older than Patricia and Eliot herself, had brought with her a breath of fresh air, an intellectual challenge, an element of transcending sophistication; but, of course, I had no way of understanding exactly why or how, since even with the help of Lori Curtis, we could not find any news regarding her person and her life.

Through the early 1970s, Eliot was more and more drawn to musing about death, the hereafter and whether or not she would live to old age. The fact that her books were out of print, that she could not publish any new work, and that she felt totally alienated from "society" made her life extremely painful.

In a loose note found among the pages of her 1971 diary she wrote:

> I have thought about this before and I believe if I only had *Hostile Country* or some stories published life would change – would look up – it always does with a book. The war books [incomprehensible words] too – even though "H.C." is a rather peculiar sort of "war" book. I can see a lot of people would dislike

---

[probably misspelled for John Heath-Stubs], Bimbo and Nicky [the cats], Dacey Gillie Conyers, Hugh Pulley & Genutlich, John Williams.

it. Though Sylvia liked it – and I trust her opinions. Anyway life would begin to "move" again if I had a book out – [incomprehensible sentence] and would bring also new and old friends into my life.

On one of those loose sheets of paper she called an "extra note", dated Sunday, 14 July, found in her 1974 diary, she expresses her dissatisfaction with people and her worries about health, and voices her need for freedom and time and quiet:

I just do not get enough time to myself. It's so difficult for me to do anything physical . . . then one's energy gets taken or when people take it as well – it's just impossible.

Also I am ill. Have been and still am in a lot of acute pain. I need some sleep . . . – quiet and freedom from interruptions. television is a terrible waste of time and most people are also a sub-normal-below par.

Her entries reflect the depressed state she and Patricia were in most of the time. She described Patricia as being in a "gloomy state" (7 January 1974), and she saw herself as living "in a state of siege" (9 January 1974) and "hollow inside" (20 April 1974). Only Sylvia knew how to comfort her when she was not well: "John came tonight but felt too ill with cold to enjoy this. P not sympathetic to my cold. Never is. Sylvia used to be very sweet when I had one. Knew how awful they were" (30 March 1974).

She seems deranged at times, her mood changing by the minute. She writes of her extra-sensorial experiences: "I was again in touch with the 'space people' [. . .] (as in 1967–1969) I asked them to make me well and strong again" (7 April 1974); she feels constantly "hollow inside" (20 April 1974).

By May 1974, however, her relationship with Patricia seems to have improved, the tension of the previous months are gone and words such as "kiss" and "love" make their appearance between the unintelligible lines of her 1970s diary: "P came in 5 to 6. tea. After Bimbo came to bed and we had love and kisses. 1st time in a long while" (7 May 1974).

Her health was improving as well, and she could even venture outdoors, to the garden, something she had not been able to do since the previous year: "Went out in the garden [. . .] first warm day Last time I went out was October on a fine warm day. Could not walk much then. walk better today" (15 May 1974).

Her regained health allowed her to see friends and there are references to frequent visits by one of her relatives, Sally Bliss, probably her niece, whom she liked a lot, and by her friend John Williams: "John came in the eve and brought a lovely pot of Chrisantemus" (26 May 1974).

She was affectionately concerned about Patricia's health and thought she should quit her job at Prior's. But days of renewed love – "P brought me a beautiful cyclamen (white) . . . it's in my room. on bookcase" (19 October 1975) – would alternate with days of deep depression in which their relationship seemed on the verge of a breakup.

Increasingly, periods of intensive work, which would make her feel inspired and alive, would alternate with periods of intense dejection, when her health would prevent her from working or going outside, or even walking; cortisone, taken to ease the pain, would cause heavy swelling, and music would be the only thing that could help her (18 July 1975).

⠿⠿⠿

Between 1975 and 1978, the death of a number of friends would darken her life, and contribute to making her feel severed from society: George Burton, friend and doctor, John Kirkwood, John Hepburn, and even her beloved cat.

On 7 January 1975 John Kirkwood made what would be his last visit, and brought her some perfumed soap and Darjeeling tea. Throughout the year she would mention his deteriorating health.

In a 25 September note, she wrote: "I rang up Sybil Kirkwood at 7.30. JK had died on Sat. 20th and was cremated [. . .]. Though I knew this was coming it is a shock and a grief [. . .]. Should ask Sybil Kirkwood for a photo of him. We have known him since 1962. I think 13 years. He was about 65 I think." And then, on the last page of her 1975 diary: "The saddest thing this year was JK's death in Sandworth of cancer. I miss him terribly." Despair and depression seem to have been her constant companions, but she was also determined to get better:

> I must be stronger and be able to work on my unfinished work. and also to walk out (go out in a car). (18 October)
> Determined to get skinnier [. . .] am determined to lose weight and get walking and go out in due course. (7 December)
> Determined (God willing) to get out of this place for a change. Next year. (19 December)

Indeed, she was a strong-willed fighter and she would eventually begin to walk again, with her "sticks", and would write more poems – one dedicated to Jessica Hepburn on her birthday – but depression and sadness were harder to shake off. She would often think of all the people she missed in her life.

> I have no friends here. And the friends I have in London I don't get on well now. I need other people to talk to occasionally. [. . .] I need at last some social intercourse. We are too isolated here. partly tho' my illness of 8 years duration. ("extra note", 18 June)
>
> thinking of my father and mother and John, my brother, and wished I had more of them whenever was possible. [. . .] perhaps [in] the end one regrets a lot of this. v. depressing. (21 October)

In 1978 she made a list of things that worried her, something about her new neighbours, and an episode regarding Sylvia and Peter Owen, the publisher. She wrote "Peter Owen (publisher) the episode about Sylvia (libel)". The librarians at Tulsa helped me with a search about libels, Sylvia and Peter Owen, but the search did not return any results, and the reason of her concern remained a mystery.

Dead people would often populate her dreams. After the description of a dream in which both her parents were present, she wrote in an extra note:

> I have been thinking about my mother lately in the day, in fact both of them, and feeling sad that I did not see none of them in later years. My father died in august 1941–1942 after an illness of 2 years. He said goodbye to me before, and said he hoped I would succeed with my work. (I cared for him a lot [. . .] and he for me).
>
> My mother died in a hospital in Kent after a stroke at the age of 80 [. . .] I was myself very ill [. . .] at the time and Patricia went to the funeral for me [. . .] in July or August 1954 – 24 years ago – I had been going to see her for five years before [. . .].
>
> My brother, John, died on Sept. 20th 1967, 11 years ago. I also cared deeply for him. I have seen "him" twice since then. I had a vision of him, while reading one night. (19–20 February 1978)

She also began regretting choices made in the past ("Thinking about my early youth [. . .] and how stupid I was then! this depressed me" (2 January);

"v. depressed today about my life and terrible waste of it in the middle years" (20 March).

In 1978 a new character appeared in her life, and seemed to bring some happiness. On 12 July she wrote "private life with Anthony Ferrara (happiness)" and then on 23 July, "Felt AF here today strongly". More references are made in 1979, after the death of another of her beloved cats, Nicky. "Re-read my write-up of AF [. . .] in Notebook and here. Only this relationship and happiness has saved me during this horrible [unintelligible]" (2 August 1979).

She kept thinking of the past, of how badly she had run her life; she also began sorting out old papers and letters, while people from the past seemed to appear in her room.

> CLG in the room [. . .]
>
> Talked to Patricia about CLG and the past but it hurt me to remember this and how stupid I was in 1934 – our last meeting. (6 December 1979)
>
> Patricia getting bad temper and worse – and makes me worse [. . .] my confidence very low [. . .]
>
> AF v. sweet and looked after me and CLG also here part of the time (11 December)
>
> I have read some of CLG's letters from 1922–23, made me terribly sad and mad with myself (13 December 1979)
>
> while he [AF] was downstairs and I ate [. . .] CLG turned up and told me he loved me. AF saw this when he came to bed. I fell asleep but when I woke up at night he held me. [. . .]
>
> AF with me while CLG in the room (20–21 December)
>
> Late at night CLG here [. . .] I had a collapse and cried – and told Patricia what life had been for me in the last 10 years (25 December)

During the first months of 1980 she kept chronicling her life with AF, even mentioning when he would go to London. I was totally baffled. She was extremely ill, the apartment was small, there could not be a "downstairs" and "upstairs", and she was living with Patricia Allan-Burns. Where did this man come from? Who was he? Was he a hallucination?

I did some search with the help of the librarians, but nowhere could we find who this person might have been. Then I noticed that all references to AF, or Anthony Ferrara, were made parenthetically, as if these passages were not part of her regular, official diary. And I understood.

AF, just as CLG, was not a real person. While CLG was a ghost, part of her past, which "now" seemed so bright, but had not actually borne any real hope for the future, AF was a complete figment of her imagination – both AF and CLG's ghost were her way to cope with the harshness of her reality.

And then I remembered what Eliot herself was quoted as saying in the introduction to the *Luminous Isle* reprint. In Jamaica she had fallen in love with a young officer, a lieutenant in the navy, and in later life she would have psychic experiences involving this young man – CLG was probably the navy officer.[11]

The diaries end with blank pages for the year 1980, with nothing after 17 July, after visions of dead people and wishes for a totally different, imagined life.

▶▶◀◀

The time to leave Tulsa came way too soon, and many of my questions remained unanswered.

I had not learned anything about Barbara or Cairn, not to mention Sylvia. The librarians at Tulsa could not find any reference to *The Albatross,* or to the actual location of the Cobden-Sanderson archive. It seemed the book never existed, or perhaps existed only in the imagination of the *Who Was Who* editors. Here was yet another mystery to be solved.

▶▶◀◀

In November 2003 I resolved to at least try to find out more about Sylvia and Peter Owen. So I contacted Ms Antonia Owen, of the Peter Owen Publishing Group, explaining that I was writing at the suggestion of Ms Lori Curtis, Head of Special Collections and Archives at the McFarlin Library, where I had the possibility of reading Eliot Bliss's diaries.

> Dear Ms Antonia Owen,
>   [. . .]
>   Indeed through her diaries I found out that she was in touch with Mr Peter Owen, that she sent some work for publication but that later their literary

---

11   Later on, I found out that CLG was Charles L. Guthrie, the young officer she was in love with.

relationship ran into some obstacles due to a possible law suit associated with Bliss's friend Sylvia Gough. Ms Bliss was actually terrified at the prospect of such suit (reported terrible nightmares about it).

I was wondering whether "Peter Owen Publishing Group" has still some of Ms Bliss's works.

Also wondering whether Mr Owen would be willing to talk to me and help shed some light on the law suit episode which, according to the entries in the diaries, haunted Ms Bliss during the last years of her life.

Please let me know whether this would be possible, and, if yes, how we could proceed.

Best regards,

Michela A. Calderaro

Ms Antonia Owen kindly answered within a couple of days, and promised to get in touch with Peter Owen. She thought he might be the only person in the company to know anything about that matter. She also enquired about the dates of the possible correspondence between Eliot and Peter Owen.

I reported that in one of Eliot Bliss's diaries I had found a note concerning an episode between Peter Owen and Sylvia Gough, related to a libel suit, which worried her a lot in 1978, and that the correspondence probably took place around that time.

Ms Owen answered that although Peter Owen's memory was very good, remembering clearly some events that took place as far back as the 1950s, he could recall neither the correspondence nor the author, nor anything related to a libel suit. She added that, over the years, they had passed on archival material to several repositories, such as the Harry Ransom Center at the University of Texas at Austin.

Unfortunately, my enquiries did not provide any concrete clues.

CHAPTER 3

※►◄※

Patricia

Bishop's Stortford
15 April 2004

"And, you see," she resumed, "I knew nothing about a sexual relationship at all. That is why my father insisted that if I took this scholarship [at London Central School of Arts], I had to find lodging with women. I was nineteen, but I was one of the most innocent nineteen-year-olds you could have imagined – in the *ways of the world* . . . So, it's very difficult to say, you just went with it . . . But of course, you see, I was with Patience and Eliot . . . Of course people fall in love with the wrong people, often . . ."

Again she looked straight into my eyes, and I felt uncomfortable. Was my curiosity impertinent? Was she resenting it? After all, I was there to learn about the literary life of Eliot Bliss, and we were talking about the beginning of their lifelong relationship.

"Mind if I smoke?" She lit a cigarette, despite her asthma.

For the first time I noticed a sound, music, coming from a radio behind me, and wondered whether my recording would come out properly.

"We got television, eventually, a large one, but she didn't really . . . I thought, you know, she might. She just watched two programmes. I think she liked just listening to the radio. Always loved music." Puffs of smoke came out of her nose; she looked at me through that bluish curtain, inquisitively.

"How did you get in touch with them?" I asked, compulsively curious.

"My father was looking for a place where I would be *safe* from the world. And my sister was then living with a writer, Kay Burdekin . . . Oh, my father was terribly strict, with all of us. But that, I suppose, was his generation, you know. But I must say being nineteen and being in a . . . uh . . . you know, I had no idea, as I said. Not long after, I realized. But it happened and that was that, so . . . here we are."

She laughed, a rumble of a laugh, heartily. I was beginning to adore her.

"Because of the way I've been brought up . . . I was born in the Church of England and one only mixed with a certain society of people . . . You never went outside that circle, at all, and one just didn't know what life really was outside. It would have been much better if we had been exposed to the world."

"Well, at the time parents tried to shield young girls," I suggested.

I listened keenly, while trying to verify that my tape-recorder was running properly – an old, small thing, with tiny cassettes – and scribbling notes on my yellow pad, all the while not wanting to miss a moment of that stare.

"It was not good really, but that was the way it was. Isobel, my elder sister, escaped, you see, because she went to college in London, so she escaped the family. She was staying with this writer, Kay Burdekin,[1] whom she had met, I think in 1926 . . . She was a pretty good writer; Isobel's daughter, Harriet, grew up with them and with Kay's daughters. I can ask Harriet if she can loan me one of Kay's books. I'll give it to you to read. I met Kay, it was only long before the war. She was very nice, she was charming. She heard that Patience and Eliot had a room to let, and that was it . . ."

"That was it?" I repeated.

---

1   Kay Burdekin (23 July 1896–10 August 1963), like Eliot Bliss, can be considered as a "neglected writer".

In 1915 she married Beaufort Burdekin and had two daughters; she later divorced him in 1922.

Her real name was Katharine Penelope Cade, but her antifascist position, her strong feminist stance, and her being a lesbian forced her to write under the male pseudonym of Murray Constantine.

Under this pseudonym she published two novels, *Proud Man* (1934) and *Swastika Night* (1937), each later reprinted under her real name in 1993 and 1985 respectively. Her novels describe a dystopian world ruled by powerful women, often forced to make heartbreaking choices. Men are always on the margins, deprived of high status.

For a thorough discussion of her works, see Daphne Patai, foreword and afterward to *Proud Man*, by Katharine Burdekin, ed. Daphne Patai (1934; repr., New York: Feminist Press, 1993); and Daphne Patai, introduction to *Swastika Night*, by Katharine Burdekin, ed. Daphne Patai (1937; repr., New York: Feminist Press, 1985). It is indeed thanks to Daphne Patai's research that the true identity of Murray Constantine was uncovered.

"But there is a difference between being strict and being so strict that you don't know what life is about . . . We had a very strict upbringing . . . Well, later on when we moved here, while my sisters and their daughters always visited me and Eliot, my brother Desmond disapproved, and never came over."

She stood up suddenly. "I'll make soup. You like soup, don't you?"

"Ah . . . eh. . . yes, of course." I do love soup. Had she offered it, though, I would have loved poison too. I followed her into the kitchen, asking whether I could help her, too late realizing she didn't need any help, certainly not mine.

"Take, you can open that bottle." She pointed at a bottle on a kitchen board.

She handed me a bottle opener, something I knew should be easy to use – easy for her perhaps, while I would probably pierce my hands and make a fool of myself. I finally made it, though, and proudly took it to the small living room, together with two glasses.

"We used to drink wine, you know. Eliot liked a little Porto in the afternoon . . . Yes, they used to drink their Porto. When I would come back from Prior's, they would be in the little room, drinking their Porto . . . Sylvia and Eliot."

I had no idea "what" Prior's was, though the name of what might have been a firm or a shop where Patricia worked appeared many times in the diaries. I wanted to ask, but I was more eager to hear about Sylvia – the *other* woman.

"Next time," I volunteered, "I'll bring some Italian wine." I would have brought her anything she asked. She didn't seem the kind of person who asked for anything, though.

"Yes . . . it will go well with my comfort soup. I can only eat soup and bread and butter, because of my stomach, you know. I had some operation."

The soup was warmly comforting me too.

"You know, I've never seen a picture of Eliot; there are no pictures anywhere. What did she look like?"

"Oh dear. Take the folder there. Yes, that one, the light brown."

She took it from my hands, and I moved near, sat on the floor.

"Here's Eliot."

At last, *she* was looking at me from a black and white photo, alive, intense and daunting, her large clear eyes piercing mine.

"Her eyes . . . What a colour! I mean, they look transparent."

"Light, almost violet," Patricia reminisced. "She would look at you with those eyes; you wouldn't cross swords with Eliot. She had a very strong . . .

an imposing personality. She frightened people, but also . . . all sorts of people loved her, often the wrong sort of people."

"Was she tall?"

"She was five feet five inches."

She handed me the folder, and I started going through the pictures.

"You were telling me about Patience Ross. Was she one of 'the wrong sort' of people?"

"No, no. Patience was very good for Eliot. I think it was Marty Mann who came between them. Eliot sort of had a passion for Marty, an American. I think that broke up the relationship with Patience. I quite honestly think it was a pity, 'cause Patience would have been a much greater companion. I don't mean in nastiness. . . . But here we are, that's her life. Patience was a poet herself. She was very talented, and she was in that world . . . the world of Eliot, where she belonged too. I think it would have been much better . . . The funny thing with Marty is that Marty was usually drunk, I'm afraid . . . But we heard later that she was running an Alcoholics Anonymous branch in America! Which I thought was terribly funny, 'cause she really was awfully naughty, Marty. She never arrived sober."

"How did she meet this Marty?"

"Oh, you just meet in London, that's what you do."

⋙⋘

I later learned Marty Mann was an attractive, impressive, wealthy socialite who had moved to London in 1930. In New York she had been working for publications such as *International Studio Magazine*, for which she wrote a column called "Seen in the Galleries". She was extremely talented, the column was a major hit and she seemed to be destined to pursue a bright career as a journalist. She was also known to be able to hold her alcohol better than anyone else. But her dream was to become a real writer, not just a journalist, and she decided the London scene would be more appropriate for her art. It was also the perfect environment where she could be herself, not needing to hide her homosexuality. Her friends belonged to the same circle as that of Eliot Bliss's – Vita Sackville-West among others. And during her frequent visits to Paris, she became friends with Natalie Barney, the feminist activist.

In Marty Mann's comprehensive biography, by Sally Brown and David R. Brown,[2] there is no mention of Eliot, nor of Anna Wickham, but it seems quite possible that Marty and Eliot shared the same circle of friends.

ANNA WICKHAM

Hove – Gruyere – London
1926–1933

Patience Ross, an editor for A.M. Heath and Co., became Eliot's agent, and lover, and had *Saraband* published by Peter Davies in 1931. The book was a success.

They had met through Anna Wickham, the poet.

Anna Wickham, whose real name was Edith Alice Mary Harper, married Patrick Hepburn, a solicitor, in 1906. Theirs was an unhappy, unfortunate marriage, and they first separated in 1926.[3]

A cousin of the Hepburns had a boarding house at Hove, Brighton; Anna went down to stay there with her two elder sons, Jim and John. Eliot, who was then recovering from one of her recurrent illnesses, was also staying there, taking a break from her job for the Encyclopaedia Britannica and a turbulent love affair. She would play table tennis with Anna's sons. Occasionally also George, the younger son, would go there.

Meeting Anna would change the course of Eliot's personal and literary career. She described her encounter with Anna in 1965, in what she later called "A First Meeting with God":

> I was in a very low and depressed state at the time, and for a week before this meeting had been taking long solitary walks in some laid out gardens not far

---

2   Sally Brown and David R. Brown, *A Biography of Mrs. Marty Mann. The First Lady of Alcoholics Anonymous* (Center City, Minn.: Hazelden, 2001).

3   Anna Wickham had been, like Eliot, extremely prolific and left behind thousands of unpublished poems. In a way, like Eliot, she can be considered a "neglected writer", having been almost ignored by critics for a long time. However, in the last decades she has been rediscovered, and it is worth mentioning that in addition to a collection of her writings – R.D. Smith, ed., *The Writings of Anna Wickham: Free Woman and Poet* (London: Virago Press, 1984), which includes a Preface by Anna's son, James Hepburn – there is a fascinating biography by Jennifer Vaughan Jones, *Anna Wickham: A Poet's Daring Life* (Lanham, NY: Madison, 2003).

away, from where I could see the sea. I felt my life to be at a very low ebb indeed, and discounted entirely – as one always does while one has – the marvellous capital of my youth. I had set out with high hopes and a higher belief in myself three years before and after leaving the University, which even repeated times of poverty and illness had failed to diminish – up to now.

[. . .]

She was tall and I thought extremely beautiful and had a deep resonant voice. She was wearing a dark green dress with a round neckline simply cut, and round her statuesque neck was a string of green beads of the same colour as the dress [. . .]. Her dark hair was done loosely round her head. Her sparkling eyes with their amused yet penetrating glance I knew closely scrutinized me, but their glance was also kind and I knew she liked me. I knew too that I was in the presence of an extraordinary person, a genius, a kind of major star, and mar-velled that everyone around did not feel the tremendous electric force which emanated from her. [. . .]

Like all people of high magnetic voltage Anna always inspired in lesser people extremes of feeling. Although I had never met it before in anyone, I immediately recognized it, and it was just what I needed. My own voltage, temporarily lowered by illness and what I now thought of as the infamous reference book, immediately rose several degrees to meet it.

[. . .]

I had met God.

[. . .]

Anna was a novelist, but the novel was being lived – Novels are not really very comfortable things to live – even though one may enjoy reading them (after all, one can close the book at any moment), living is the inescapable novel which only ends with one's death – and sometimes has repercussions for other people after that.

[. . .]

[F]or me the world because of and through her opened and flowered.[4]

Anna took under her protective wing the younger author, whose sensibility and struggle with her sexual identity seemed, in a way, to mirror her own. Was this the beginning of a mother–daughter relationship? Perhaps it was much more, and more complex.

---

4   Eliot Bliss, "A First Meeting with God", memoir of Anna Wickham, August 1965. The British Library. Courtesy of the Hepburn–Wickham family and the Eliot Bliss Estate.

In 1929, sensing that Eliot needed to break away, once again, from London, from a distractive circle of friends and from a havoc-wreaking situation, Anna introduced her to Romer Wilson and her husband, Edward O'Brien. The couple invited Eliot to stay with them in Switzerland for six months. At the Hotel Fleur-de-Lys, in the company of a writer she admired, she could enjoy the quiet and intellectual atmosphere that enabled her to finish *Saraband*.

Upon her return to England, however, the search for a publisher and the rejection of her book by Chatto and Windus sank Eliot into yet another bout of depression, from which, once again, Anna rescued her. Eliot did not have an agent, and would not know how to contact one, so Anna thought of Patience Ross, a friend who was part of Natalie Barney's circle, and a poet herself, who was also an agent.

It was a marvel of a rescue, leading Eliot to Patience Ross and, at least for a while, to a period of productive rest. Eliot and Patience fell in love and moved in together. Not only did Patience have the book published by Peter Davies in 1931, but also she had A.M. Heath hire Eliot as a reader.

Patience, whose full name was Patience Henrietta May Ropes (1906–c.1988), was the daughter of Arthur Reed Ropes (1859–1933), better known as Adrian Ross, "a very famous theatre man [. . .] who was a leading theatre personality of England". As a pen name, Patience chose her father's pseudonym, Ross. "Adrian Ross began his career as a Cambridge University don, teaching history and poetry. However, he is much better known as a writer of popular lyrics, contributing songs to British musical comedies at the Gaiety, Daly's, the Adelphi, and other London theatres."[5]

According to scholar Fiona Richards, the circle of friends and neighbours that Patience's family would host at 31 Addington Road, Kensington, included intellectuals and public figures such as Chaim Weizmann and John Galsworthy.[6]

She was not only a beautiful and talented poet, but also a piano player, a

---

5 "Alan Bush", in *The John Ireland Companion: Interviews with Friends and Contemporaries of Ireland*, ed. Lewis Foreman (Woodbridge, Suffolk: Boydell, 2011), 69.

6 Fiona Richards has created a thorough and informative site dedicated to English composer John Ireland (1879–1962): https://johnirelandmusicpeopleplaces.wordpress.com/2014/04/28/irelands-books-patience-ross/.

pupil of John Ireland, to whom she dedicated her first book of poems, *Black Bread* (1929).[7] By that date she had already begun working for A.M. Heath and Co. She had in fact joined the agency in 1926, at the age of twenty-two, as a typist, soon to begin acting as an agent.

Her love for music led her to write the lyrics for "Earth Does Not Hold: Hymn for Armistice Day", set to music by Eric Thiman,[8] probably around 1928, and then *The Captive: A Romany Operetta* (1934), with music by Edgar Moy (1893–1973), "a pianist and organist who wrote a mixture of light music and organ works".[9]

Her second book of poems, *The Glass Rose* (1930),[10] is dedicated to Audrey Heath.

The sentimental and economic tranquillity bore some fruits, and eventually enabled Eliot to finish her second novel, *Luminous Isle*. Just when she was hoping Patience would again act as her agent, however, their love life at 1A Hill Side Road was coming to an end.

Eliot, then an acclaimed new voice in 1930s London elite literary circles, and a scandal in the lesser known, lesbian clubs, would turn to loyal Patricia Allan-Burns.

⤐⤏

The friendship with the Hepburn–Wickham family continued, even after Anna's suicide in 1947.[11] Anna's sons, Jim and George Hepburn, kept visiting

---

7   Patience Ross, *Black Bread* (Oxford: Basil Blackwell, 1929).

8   Paul Minchinton, EDOA Newsletter, September 2015, www.edoa.org.uk. According to Minchinton, "Given that it was probably written during or just after the First World War, it is interesting to note the tone of the poem which forms the text of this anthem. Unlike many such before or since it shows no jingoism, is not triumphalist and does not glorify warfare. Rather, it expresses faith that those who fight and fall are gathered into a new and better place to which we can all aspire."

9   "Ireland's Books: Patience Ross", *John Ireland: Music, People, Places*, 28 April 2014, https://johnirelandmusicpeopleplaces.wordpress.com/2014/04/28/irelands-books-patience -ross/.

10   Patience Ross, *The Glass Rose* (Oxford: Basil Blackwell, 1930).

11   As discussed by Jennifer Vaughan Jones (*Anna Wickham*, 219), Anna had already tried to take her life in 1930, only to be saved by her son Jim. Her unhappy life and her recurrent depression were well known by her friends, and made clear in her "Life Story", a forty-nine-page unpublished poem, written either in February or March 1939 and analysed by

and writing to Eliot frequently. In one of her "extra notes", dated 30–31 December, found among the pages of her 1974 diary, Eliot described her relationship with the Wickham–Hepburn family: "Awake in the early hours, I think how my relationship with the Hepburn family is an 'organic one' similar to a family tree. In one way I need them in my life. Perhaps they too, to some extent – feel this about me. Because of Anna – and also because of our long association from youth to now."[12] Then she added, "I was in a state of anguish when I wrote this."

On the evening of Tuesday, 31 December, George Hepburn rang her up to wish a happy new year, and on 29 December, so did his brother, Jim. The reason for her anguish is not explained.

S U S A N

Bishop's Stortford
15 April 2004

Before meeting Anna, Bliss's years in London were highlighted by her friendship with Susan Curtnoys, the girl she had become close to in the Highgate convent. Susan would later study at the Royal College of Music, while Eliot completed her education at University College London, studying journalism. In the beginning both girls would stay with Susan's mother, Mrs Lewis. Then they moved together into a studio apartment.

Patricia remembered Susan vividly. She made me *see* how she must have looked. "She had beautiful hands . . . beautiful hands. I remember Susan coming down to Clifton Gardens. They've always kept in touch through the years. Oh, beautiful Susan. She married five times." Patricia lit another cigarette, coughing throughout. "I got emphysema, you know. I need this little thing

---

Vaughan Jones (248–50, 258, 272). Then, "On the 30th of April, 1947, Wednesday, a spring day after the worst winter in recent memory, Anna told George [her son] to go out. She was in a good, possibly great mood. [. . .] When he let himself back it was nearly night [. . .]. When he did not see her [. . .] he thought with pleasure that she had gone to the Fitzroy – a good sign, since there she met friends and had a good time. But when he turned, he saw that his mother had hanged herself from the frame of the full-length French windows" (269).

12   "The Eliot Bliss Diaries", entry dated 31 December 1974 (Special Collections, McFarlin Library, Tulsa University).

here." She pointed at something that looked like a spray bottle, the spray I had seen before on the small table.

"Susan was so beautiful. And Eliot – they must have been absolutely fabulous together. They used to go to the Henry Wood's concert in the old days. They used to go to promenade concerts. I'd love to have seen them together, walking through the park. Susan was a wonderful pianist but . . . John Alland was a great friend of hers, she was his *protégé*. He wrote a piano concerto, and he wanted her to play it, but she couldn't. She could not perform on a platform. She would go into a stage-fright . . . Tragic really, because she just couldn't . . . Awful really. And with her looks it would have been wonderful. But there you are, two convent girls. Dear, oh dear . . ."

⟫⟪

Eliot finally moved out of the studio apartment she shared with Susan Curtnoys, and whose friendship had suffered a severe blow by Eliot's first turbulent, heartbreaking, on-and-off love affair. Had Eliot been in love with Susan? Was this the real reason for the breakup? In the autobiographical *Saraband*, the underlying homosexuality of the characters is never spelled out. Yet it is tangible, and later, in *Luminous Isle*, the sexual tension between the two girls made clear in the most delicate way: "Another veil touched her own on the rail. Without looking she was immediately aware of Œnone's body. The sudden restless movement of the hands stretched over the rail saying her rosary – the bowed head under the white veil, the light sea-green eyes, the soft, very soft hair touching her cheek in the semi-darkness" (*Luminous,* 50).

"Patricia, in the book *Saraband,* she describes her family," I noted. "She seems to have been very fond of a cousin who would play the piano. Do you have any idea who this cousin might have been, whether he actually existed, or was he just a literary invention?"

No, Patricia had never heard of any cousin who played the piano. Possibly, then, Susan had also inspired the figure of the boy.

"In *Saraband* she also describes her friends. One character is a clear portrait of Susan, but then there is another girl who seems to be just as important."

"In the convent there was a Betty Fleishoff. And there were the nuns. They were also important to Eliot. She used to go back to see them."

"Her novels are definitely autobiographical. Did Eliot tell you about the persons she described in *Luminous Isle*?"

"In Jamaica there were the Farquarsons. They were very important for her. Mr Farquarson would let her use his car. She had not passed the test, but he let her drive his car.

"And May, the daughter, came here a few times, to see Eliot, long after the war. She had a sister . . . I think there was a sister. . . . They were very important people on the island. Both the father and May would come to visit occasionally, and they all used to take Eliot out.

"May's home was in Jamaica. She did a lot of work for the poor. She was charming, but rather severe. She was very much given to good work. That was her life, you know. She did a great deal in Jamaica.

"There was this nice person Eliot was engaged to. His family was in the grapefruit business. He must have been very nice to tell her to do what she wanted. He knew she wanted to go to university and said, 'You must go, and then come back and we'll be married.' Then, when Eliot went back she went into a different life, because she had grown up. But the Farquarsons were always very important to her.

"She didn't want to live the 'colony's daughter' sort of life she was expected to but rebelled against. Yes, I can understand it. It must have been a very rigid life, you know. And also, she loved the people. She liked being with them . . .'"

"Are you tired?" I asked her. We had been talking for a long time, and I felt it was time for me to leave.

"Yes. . . . I'm going to rest a bit and read the paper. Shall I see you tomorrow, say ten o'clock?"

"Sure," I said, thankful for the invitation.

"We'll have another type of soup, with tomatoes, a new one I've never tried before. You know the way through the garden, right? Bye, dear. See you tomorrow. . . . And take the folder, the letters and the pictures. It's for you."

I had met her only a few hours earlier, but I hugged and kissed her like an old friend.

I found my way out, of course, and sat in the garden a while, cats looking at me, strolling by, while I opened the folder and began to read, letters, pages . . . thinking how peculiar everything was turning out to be.

Upon my return from Tulsa, I had written again, twice, to Patricia, and she had never answered. Then one afternoon, out of frustration, I had looked up Bishop's Stortford on the Internet, then wrote to the town library, the office of the mayor and even the local history museum – not expecting much, just to make sure I didn't leave any stone unturned.

FINDING PATRICIA

30 March 2004

The site of the Local History Museum (Cemetery Lodge, Apton Road, Bishop's Stortford) listed as the person to be contacted for information the curator, the Honourable W.J. Wright. So I wrote my email, explaining who I was and the reason of my enquiry, and specifying that since the last known address for Patricia Allan-Burns and Eliot Bliss was in Bishop's Stortford (152 Plaw Hatch Close), I was hoping he could help me find out who currently held the rights to Ms Bliss's estate and writings, and where her letters and manuscripts might physically be; as well as, possibly, share his ideas as to where Ms Bliss's friend, Ms Patricia Allan-Burns, may reside at present.

The day after, I received an informative and helpful answer.

> From: Hannah Kay[13]
> To: Michela A. Calderaro
> Subject: Re: Eliot Bliss
> Date: 31 March 2004
>
> Dear Michela,
>   Thank you for your enquiry regarding Eliot Bliss. Mr Wright retired as Honorary Curator a few years ago when the Local History Museum merged with the town's Rhodes Museum. My name is Hannah Kay. I am Curator of the new Bishop's Stortford Museum. I will search our archive for any information on Eliot or Eileen Bliss.
>   I have also contacted our county archive. They are searching their local records for any information about Eliot Bliss, her life in Bishop's Stortford or her publications. I have also contacted the British Library in London – they

---

13   I wish to thank Ms Hannah Kay for her help. All efforts have been made to reach her after I finished this book, but she had left Bishop's Stortford, and the new curator could not give me any forwarding address for her.

hold a copy of every book ever published in the UK, so hopefully they may be able to find evidence of her other writings.

I will contact you again as soon as I have any information.

Thank you for your enquiry, I wish you every success with your interesting research.

Best wishes,

Hannah Kay

From: Hannah Kay
To: Michela A. Calderaro
Subject: Re: Eliot Bliss
Date: 31 March 2004

Dear Michela,

Just to let you know 'Eliot Bliss' is listed in our latest 2004/2005 Telephone Directory as still living at 152 Plaw Hatch Close Bishop's Stortford Tel: 01279 651766. This seems very strange as you say she died there in 1990.

Do you want to call this number? Do you want me to call this number – maybe it is a relative? Maybe they will know more information about her?

Let me know.

Best wishes,

Hannah Kay

From: Michela A. Calderaro
To: Hannah Kay
Subject: Re: Eliot Bliss
Date: 1 April 2004

Dear Hannah,

Thanks a lot for your prompt response. You gave an immense boost to this project, to our quest for Eliot Bliss's lost manuscripts and biographical details.

Eliot Bliss and Patricia Allan-Burns moved to Bishop's Stortford in the 1950s. My hope is that Patricia, who gave the Diaries to McFarlin through a book-dealer, and was much younger than Eliot, might still be alive.

Indeed I once wrote to her at 152 Plaw Hatch Close, but my letters were never answered nor returned. Eliot had a niece, Sally Bliss, daughter of her brother, John, but I wasn't able to trace her either.

My only source of information are the Diaries, 19 volumes densely written in obscure handwriting. As far as I know I am the only scholar actually working on Eliot Bliss.

I was tempted to immediately pick up the phone and dial that number you sent me, but then I thought the current residents at 152 Plaw Hatch Close might be alarmed to hear someone with a foreign accent asking questions about a person who no longer lives there. So, if you are willing to make that phone call and let them know I will be calling later, I would be immensely grateful.

Thanks for your gracious help.

Best wishes,

Michela Calderaro

From: Hannah Kay
To: Michela A. Calderaro
Subject: Made contact with Patricia Allan-Burns!!
Date: 1 April 2004

Dear Michela,

I've had a very exciting morning!

I phoned the number listed for Eliot Bliss – it rang and rang, then was answered and went dead. I tried again and an elderly sounding lady answered (very out of breath). She was Patricia Allan-Burns. I introduced myself as the local museum curator and she was aware of our museum and stayed on the line. I said I had an enquiry from an academic in Italy researching Eliot Bliss's writings and would she consider taking a phone call from you to discuss Eliot's work. She has agreed and is expecting your call.

I said you had travelled to McFarlin University and had read the diaries but needed more information about her books, plays and poems. She is more than happy to help you with your work.

I would let the phone ring a long time as I think it takes her a while to answer.

I have been sent information from the British Library about existing copies of *Saraband* and *Luminous Isle*. There are early 1930s copies at Oxford and Cambridge University libraries – you will find details on the COPAC website www.copac.ac.uk.

They give date of publication, location etc.

The British Library had no records of any other publications by Eileen or Eliot Bliss.

Please let me know how you get on. I specialise in Imperial and African history (our museum holds a collection of African artwork and items relating to Cecil Rhodes). On an unprofessional note, *Wide Sargasso Sea* and *Jane Eyre* are amongst my favourite books. I would love to know what information you uncover!

Best wishes,

Hannah

To: Hannah Kay

Subject: Re: Made contact with Patricia Allan-Burns!!

Date: 1 April 2004

Dear Hannah,

How could I ever thank you enough?

I have just talked to Patricia Allan-Burns. Indeed she sounded old, but happy to talk. I didn't think it was proper for me to start inquiring about lost manuscripts and details of Eliot's life, but I asked her whether she would be willing to see me and we agreed that I would be in Bishop's Stortford immediately after the Easter vacation.

We also agreed that I would send her a letter, confirming our meeting and that I would call her again once I have the exact dates of my stay in Bishop's Stortford.

It is all so exciting and your help has been enormous.

I will let you know the dates in which I plan to be in Bishop's Stortford and perhaps I can stop by once I'm there (primarily to thank you in person).

Thanks for your most gracious help.

Best wishes,

Michela

5 April 2004

Dear Ms Patricia Allan-Burns,

I wish to thank you for talking to me on the telephone and for agreeing to meet me. It means a lot to me.

As we agreed I will be travelling to Bishop's Stortford after Easter. I plan to arrive on the 15th of April and stay for a few days (until 19th of April).

I will try to call you after arriving. I hope you will be able to see me.

My greatest hope is to revive interest in Ms Eliot Bliss and her writings. As you know, I've been studying Ms Bliss for years and admire her work.

Thanks again for your graciousness.

Regards,

Michela A. Calderaro

≫≪

I let the phone ring for a long, long time. Then a deep, resonant voice answered at the other end.

"Hello . . ."

"Hi, my name is Michela Calderaro. I'm calling from Italy. May I speak to Ms Allan-Burns?"

"Yes, this is she."

"You have probably talked to Ms Hannah Kay, from the museum."

"Yes."

"I'm working on Ms Eliot Bliss's novels and was wondering whether you would agree to see me, just to talk."

"When do you want to come? I'm very old, you know, I'm almost ninety – you shouldn't wait too long."

My throat was like parchment, the receiver all sweaty, and I didn't know what to answer.

"Would it be fine with you if I come over immediately after Easter?"

"Let me check on my calendar."

The voice disappeared for a long time, and I heard noises.

"Yes," she resumed. "But my sister is coming to see me on the 19th . . ."

I thought quickly. I could not disturb her for more than a couple of days. She said she was old. Well, she *was* old. Maybe I would have to let her rest in between our meetings . . .

"It would have to be before then. What about Thursday, the 15th?"

"Good, I'll be waiting for you. You give me a call when you get here. You have a hotel?"

"No, but I'll get one, and I will also write to you, with the exact date and time."

"Bye, dear."

"Bye then. And thank you so much."

It took me some time to return to reality and put down the receiver.

Indeed, the telephone call, though brief, had left me in a state of euphoria. I had talked to Eliot's companion, the woman who probably knew her better than anybody else in the world, and I was going to find out who were all the people mentioned in the diaries; perhaps what had happened to her writings, too.

Perhaps she even knew where the lost manuscripts were.

⊱⊱⊱⊰⊰⊰

I went back to Pearce House that night, my heart pounding. It was something I had not expected; Patricia Allan-Burns had given me a whole bunch of letters and Eliot's pictures. I felt dizzy. After so many years, I could look at Eliot, read her correspondence.

Eating was out of the question that night; I made tea, pots of tea. I sat on the bed, letters spread all over, with the beautiful picture of Eliot, framed in old, dark metal, in front of me. A night of amazement began.

I sorted the material into small piles, according to dates, then according to signatures at the bottom of letters, and then I began to read. There were letters from publishers and female friends, some urging her to leave Patricia, offering to support her and make a home together; there were invitations to parties. A letter from Vita Sackville-West. Some letters referred to Sylvia, the mysterious Sylvia, but did not shed any light on who she was and why she was living with Eliot and Patricia.

I read through the night, transported to another world, dancing at parties, sharing a comment on a new play or on a new 1920s London fashion. Some of the names were familiar, while others were totally unknown. There were letters from Barbara Wand, probably the same Barbara who was mentioned in the diaries; letters from a Danny Gilbert; from someone called Victor; and a few letters, signed "Stephen", were unmistakably love letters.

I knew, from what I had read in the introduction to *Luminous Isle*, that she had had a fiancé back in Jamaica, but it was clear, to anybody who read *Saraband*, that her homosexuality was unshakable and unquestionable.

How was it then, that in the late 1920s she was having what appeared to have been a stormy affair with this man Stephen? The first letter I read from him was double-folded in a blank envelope, covered by a small neat handwriting:

> I suppose it is my fault. I'm sorry I've made you so unhappy . . . but don't you see – it will always be more or less like this. When I'm in a good mood and we are getting on well together – of course everything seems as if it will always be

alright – but you are right, we are "poles apart". – I'm a bloody little neurotic, and I make you as bad.

You are probably right about all the things you say of me – I suppose, I love you, really, but it doesn't seem to make any difference – I don't think it will be "love" that will pull our relationship together – if anything does, which I doubt.

This sounds beastly – I'm sorry I really wanted to write you something nice . . . but I seriously think we'll be better friends if we didn't live together. You'll never work while you are being upset by me, and one thing you are quite wrong in thinking – is – that I don't want you to write. I do – it's one of the things – perhaps the only thing, that will ever make you very happy. You need a person too – but I'll never do, because I'm not reliable enough – and because I'm all the things you say I am.

My dear, do you know I began to write this because I wanted to write you something to make you happier . . . and this is what I've written, and somehow I can't say anything else – I do want you to be happy, too.

Stephen

Besides this letter, with no date or address, there were other three letters from Stephen: one postmarked 21 April 1929, another 28 September 1930; and yet another, from Menton, dated 27 April 1932, which was more like a friend's letter, describing an adventurous trip to Monte Carlo. Stephen was travelling with a girl whom Eliot must have known. The letters bearing dates must have been written after the separation, though, since the tone is different, no longer that of a lover.

Who *was* Stephen, and what was Eliot doing in those years? Had she already begun writing *Saraband*?

〰〰

16 April 2004

"I've been reading the letters through the night. Really. I didn't sleep. There are so many things that I don't understand. There are many love letters, and letters from literary people . . ."

"Tell me, dear," said Patricia. "Maybe I know some of those people."

"There's an invitation by Monica Wakely, to 'Eliot Bliss and friend' to a party. Then another card, by Wakely, a 1932 Christmas card."

"Yes, Eliot had a job as her chauffeur. She was thinking of becoming a member of Parliament. She didn't succeed, but for a period of time, Eliot chauffeured her."

"There are some letters from Danny Gilbert, Victor, Barbara Wand . . ."

"Ah, Danny Gilbert was one of her friends from the Air Force at Spellbrook. He was in the Air Force and was stationed up the lane. There were Harold, and Victor. . . . They were the true naughty boys. They would rush to London when they were not supposed to go! They were often in the cottage. Barbara . . . she remained friends till she died. She was . . . she used to spend a lot of time in the cottage . . ."

"Eliot seems to be very fond of her."

"Barbara had a sort of sad life. Her mother had died in 1918, during the flu, and she was brought up by her grandmother, who was a lovely person, but she had this lonely childhood, you know. Eliot's friendship meant a lot to her . . . for both of them."[14]

"Patricia, there's one thing, though, that is puzzling me. I thought Eliot, you know . . . After we talked yesterday, I had the feeling she was not so interested in men. Then I read these letters from . . ."

"Queer. That's how they would call us then. Eliot fell in love with men too. There was this old gentleman in Jamaica, and a younger officer, and the Navy boys. There are pictures in the folder I gave you . . ."

"Ah, I understand." Or at least I thought I did. "Then this Stephen was . . ."

"Steve. Naughty Steve! The wicked Steve. . . . Picked all of them. Wouldn't miss a girl. A real troublemaker. . . . It was because of Steve, I guess, that Eliot moved out of the studio she was sharing with Susan."

So it was not because of her first, real affair with a woman, as I had wrongly inferred. It was because of Stephen.

"All this was taking place in the circle of Anna Wickham's friends?"

"No, no, dear. I wouldn't think Anna was . . . Anna's circle was more literary. The others . . . there was Bosom Kate, you know. . . . They would meet

---

14 Patricia and I met many times over the years, and she donated to me more letters from Eliot's friends. Many of these were from Barbara, and they show how Barbara was torn between Eliot and Pat – going so far as begging Eliot to let go of Pat, so that she and Pat could build a new life together. I doubt Pat was ever aware of the feelings Barbara had for her; in Pat's life there was room only for Eliot.

near Crosby Hall. There was Eileen Power, who was a professor at some university – I don't know what her specialty was, because Eliot said she had the most beautiful Chinese costumes, you know, really beautiful. In any case, there was Anna, *then* there was the Steve crowd. They were all sort of . . . dear, oh dear. That is why Anna got Eliot away to Switzerland, 'cause she was in a terrible state, and it was through Anna that Eliot met Romer Wilson. Anna was determined to break it up, because Steve was creating a great deal of upsetting turmoil. . . . That's how it happened, dear. The main thing was going to Switzerland with Romer Wilson, to take her away from Steve.

"She spent nine months there, in 1929, at the Hotel Fleur-de-Lys. She made friends there. There was a nice maid she kept a correspondence with. When she came back, Romer gave her some little money to allow her to finish, you know, the book. Romer Wilson was very tragic. She died of cancer; she was married to Edward O'Brien, and they had one son. After Romer's death, Eliot and Edward kept writing to each other."

So it was in the Stephen's aftermath that Eliot met Patience Ross.

⋙⋘

"*Why* do you really want to know about Eliot?"

Patricia had just returned from the kitchen, where the "new" soup was simmering, parsley and tomato fragrances quietly invading the small apartment.

"I found her book, *Saraband*, in a second-hand bookstore, in New York, years ago, and out of curiosity I tried to find some articles or books about her work in the library, and there was none. On the book cover there was a note saying she had adopted the name "Eliot" when she moved to England, but there was no mention of her birth name. It all began like a mystery. The more I was trying to find out about her, the more frustrated I became."

"She received letters from scholars who wanted to write about her books, but nobody actually did. She should have probably remained in London, in her world, where she would meet people and make contacts. . . . Poor Eliot."

"Pat, going back to the letters, can you tell me about Steve?"

"Oh, dear, oh dear; Baker Quinn, who introduced Cairn to Eliot . . ." She took a deep breath.

Cairn – I was going to discover more about Cairn and Steve.

"Baker Quinn, I was saying, later on ended up with Steve, and they lived in Menton, and they said that Steve was wonderful during the war. . . . Held everybody together. I've never known the real names. They all had nicknames. . . . They were all, you know. . . . Dickson would become Dickie. In those days, apart from Radclyffe Hall, people didn't *dress*, but everyone knew. You sort of recognized it. They didn't dress in any man's way; the only one was Oliver Marston, but you wouldn't have known that she wasn't a man, no. She was a good friend of Eliot. It's not that she dressed *queer*, she dressed as a man. Most queers in those days did not. It wasn't like Radclyffe Hall. It wasn't flamboyant. It didn't seem necessary to . . . they didn't make a point, it was part of life. The whole point . . . it was far worse for men. They had a very difficult time. It's an awful thing. Eliot knew Radclyffe Hall and Una Troubridge . . ."

"And Steve . . ."

"Ah, Steve's letter. Eliot was in such a state. Anna. . . . Anna rescued her. Steve. . . . No, I've never known *her* real name."

Literary Circles and Others

"So, on the one hand, there were Anna Wickham and Dorothy Richardson . . ."

"Oh, yes, Dorothy Richardson was lovely. Anna Wickham and Dorothy Richardson and her husband, that was a whole literary world, you know. And the poets and writers. . . . No, Baker Quinn and Cairn was a different age, dear."

"Which period are we talking about, with Baker Quinn and these other friends?"

Quinn and Cairn, again.

"We were in Clifford Road then. And, you see, Eliot went to America, and came back. We first started off in this one-bedroom apartment in Douglas Road. But we moved to Warwick Avenue, because that was not . . . because I had a bed in the kitchen, you know. So we had a flat in Warwick Avenue, and then of course the war. . . . So that was a different period."

"Anna. . . . We are talking about the 1930s?"

"I can't remember. She went to America twice, and probably the second time was '37, and the first time '35/'36 – you'll find out. You see, as soon as Cairn appeared, that was, you know, that was what was important to Eliot. It was Cairn. Anna was an earlier period. Eliot knew Anna when her husband died. She . . . 'cause I didn't know Eliot then, you see."

Cairn, again.

"When you met Eliot, you were very young."

"Yes, but I know how important that period was. Anna was the *one* person .. Anna was an incredible person, she was . . . she threatened the life out of me. Dynamic. If Anna was around, it was . . . uh! electric. She had *that thing*, yes.

"It was so tragic that she took her life. Dreadful. She'd been through the war. Her two boys were in the Service, and she never knew where they were. It must have been terrible. George was in the Service, the other two boys were always abroad. It must have been a great strain. And she probably wasn't eating properly, you know. When Eliot went up there, people told her, Anna would go wandering . . . sitting on the pavement . . . It must have been dreadful. The whole world had fallen apart, you know. I mean most of her friends would have been in the Service one way or another. A time for her very hard . . . She would be walking in Hampstead.

"It was dreadful for George. . . . It was George who found her. . . . He is such a sweet person. . . . Are you also going to see the Hepburns?"

"I'd love to, but I will have to do it next time. Right now I can only stay a few days. I'm going back to Italy on Monday."

"Let's have a look at the soup. It should be ready."

I helped like the day before, and we finished the bottle of wine with the tomato soup. White wine. I took a note of it, for my next visit.

I cleared the table and put the plates in the kitchen, but was forbidden from washing anything; she would take care of the sink later on. We sat quietly again while the classical music was making me feel at home. I looked around. The room was quite messy, but not that different from my own studio: piles of books and papers all over, pictures hanging here and there, small bookcases full of volumes, standing or laid horizontally to make them fit, two enormous vases with dry flowers placed in the corners of the room, a felt hat, and a beautiful painting hanging over Patricia's bed.

She followed my eyes. "That's *Rebekkah*. I can keep the painting until I die. Jo Jones [V.M. Jones] did it.[15] It was supposed to be on the book jacket

---

15   Jo Jones, as reported in Alexandra Pringle's introduction, was professionally known as V.M. Jones.

for *Luminous Isle*, but it didn't. The book jacket was done by Tony Bradshaw, who had been in Jamaica with Jones . . . When I die, someone will have it."

She sounded hurt. Some sad memory had probably surfaced, and this made me aware that the talk was becoming too personal, thought it had nothing to do with my research on the works of Eliot Bliss. I didn't ask who would get the painting.

CHAPTER 4

⋙⋘

The Vanished Works

Bishop's Stortford
17 April 2004

The morning after, we were both in a less sombre mood.

It was a beautiful day, cold and crisp. The sun was shining over the garden, and the herbs yielded a strong fragrance. I tried to imagine what Eliot must have seen when she would look out the window of her small room. In her diaries she mentioned the roses and other flowers, as well as cats baking in the sun or chasing birds.

The door was open, and Patricia called me from the living room. There was a lady who had just finished doing her hair and was saying goodbye. I was to learn that Patricia had a person coming in every week to help her take a bath and dry her hair. She smelled perfumed and looked beautiful.

I took out my notes. I didn't feel it was proper going into Eliot's ties with Sylvia, Marty or Cairn again, so I decided to talk about her diaries.

"The diaries kept at McFarlin begin in 1959. The years 1961 and 1962 are missing. And the last one is of 1980. There are no diaries covering earlier and later years."

"In this flat we've lived for thirty-six years, here in Bishop's Stortford. I don't know. . . . For many years I had to buy her a one-page diary at Christmas. I don't know when she started. I've never read her diaries. It was private."

"Her writing is very difficult to understand. Most of her personal ideas and feelings are scribbled on small notes, little pieces of paper, stuck between the pages. . . . It would have been interesting to decipher everything, but I simply couldn't. What I understood is that she was working extensively on poems, novels, plays, short stories. . . . She often wrote things like 'worked a lot on', with the title of what she worked on. She would also draw a little 'W' next to the title. There are so many things, and I was wondering whether any of these titles mean anything to you. *The Other World* (1968), which is probably a play, *The Dispossessed* (written in 1955, but revised in 1964), 'Blowing Up for Rain' . . ."

"Is that a poem? The title sounds like a poem, isn't it?"

"There are many other titles of short stories and poems. . . . In the 1966 diary she mentions she found her old manuscript of *The Father of His [?] Children*. Then between 1963 and 1967 she was writing *Telepathic Signals*, probably about some extra-terrestrial experience . . ."

A big smile lit her face. "Oh, yes, she had become interested in the flying objects . . . 'cause at one time both Sylvia and Eliot had become very interested in flying objects, and she knew this couple, Collins something and his wife – he is the person who took the beautiful pictures of the cats, he was a photographer – they used to come and they were all terrible believers in extra-terrestrials. And she was interested in that, very interested in people coming from other planets. This couple, they eventually went to live in Wales. Flying saucers. . . . Oh, yes. Sylvia and Eliot, for quite a period of time. . . . Come with me."

We visited the backroom, where, she said, Sylvia would stay. A tiny, cozy room.

"They would sit there, and they were really interested, and I got books on it, you know. I haven't got them here. The lady who came here, she was very interested, so I gave her the books on the space people."

We went back to the living room, and I took a look at my notes again. I wanted to ask about Sylvia, but the mystery of the vanished works was more pressing at the moment.

"There's a novel she was very happy about," I said. "She wrote – if I got it right – that it was 'a sort of war novel', but was not specific about it. She had revised it many times and finally it was ready. The title was *Hostile Country*. And there was a play too. She would mark the days she worked on it with a big 'W' and a small crown on top. It was called *Seti*, on some Egyptian king. *Seti* is mentioned a number of times in her diaries."

In the 1966 diary, for instance, there was a note that read:

At the Court of Seti
A dedication to play
For Seti
"Beloved of Ptah"
Who brought me peace
from the Ancient World
Oct. 29 1966

"Of course I remember *Hostile Country*; I tied it up with a blue, beautiful ribbon, as I always did with her books. And the play *Seti* – I got many books for her, from the library and also from London. I remember she worked a lot on *Seti*. She was happy with the play. All those books I brought home for her research . . ."

"Do you remember what these works were about?"

"I would not read her works. I would not interfere with her literary life. It was her private life. . . . *Hostile Country* was probably about this place. She never liked Bishop's Stortford."

"Do you know what happened to this novel, or to other works she mentions in her diaries?"

I pressed her, so full of expectations that I almost dropped my notes on the floor. I was going to find out what had happened to the lost works of Eliot Bliss. My treasure hunt was nearly over. I knew I should have been less direct and not press an old lady, but . . .

"I have no idea. I have never read the diaries. I've no idea what's in there. I wouldn't . . . I don't know what happened to her works. They're not here."

Not here. My heart lost a beat. And then another.

"In her diaries she says she is concerned about her manuscripts. She says she does not trust the home helper. She actually sounds very worried, writes that she has to hide what she writes, or what she is revising, because she fears someone might displace her work, or steal it."

"Oh dear, we always had nice home helpers."

"Well, there's also one thing that is puzzling me: the diaries end abruptly."

"It doesn't give us any hint or clues?"

"No, nothing."

"What else she says? Maybe we can find out."

"Well," I said, "she was so concerned about people touching her notes that she resorted to hiding the manuscripts every night, when she would finish her revisions. Sometimes in a drawer, sometimes under her bed in a box, or a briefcase."

"Oh, dear, oh dear. Under her bed. . . . Her last years she wouldn't move from the bed; she was suffering from arthritis, and was almost blind."

"Yes, but I'm talking about the years before 1980, when the diaries stop."

"I see. I would have found the manuscripts after her death, if they were here."

If they were here, but they weren't.

The soup was brewing in the kitchen, and its new fragrance was pervading the room. Leek and potato soup, her "comfort soup".

The realization that no manuscripts had been kept here shattered my hopes. And she could see it.

"I'll get the soup. You can take the bread and butter."

I did as ordered and felt warmer inside.

Over the soup we discussed again the mystery of the vanished works. She couldn't understand, and neither did I, where they might have ended up or who might have taken them.

"Anything else you want to know, dear?"

I needed to wash my hands before resuming our talk, so I excused myself and went to the little bathroom, in front of Eliot's room.

When I came out – it had taken me a couple of minutes – she was gone. I heard her voice but couldn't understand where it was coming from.

"Michela, dear, can you help me, please. . . . Help . . ."

She was not in the kitchen, not in the living room. I began to panic. Then pushed open the door to Eliot's room. She was on the floor, on all fours, panting badly. God, I prayed, please don't let her die in my arms, please.

"It's heavy, and I cannot pull it out," she said. And breathed a sigh of relief.

She was trying to haul something from under the bed. I helped her to her feet and led her to the armchair in the living room.

"Patricia, don't move. I'll take care of whatever is there. Breathe slowly. I'll get you some water. You need anything for your asthma?"

She didn't look well but waved me imperiously to go back and do what I was supposed to do.

The trunk was heavy indeed. I had no idea how she could possibly have moved it. I was having some difficulty myself. I dragged it to the living room.

We were both thrilled – what kind of surprise were we going to unwrap?.

"Open it," she said.

The old lock offered some resistance but finally opened. Dust, folders, a moth-eaten dusty scarf, parcels, something *soft* wrapped in whitish paper, more dust.

"Take out everything. Put it on the floor."

I was on my knees, covered with dust, and took out one item after another.

"This is silverware. Cups, saucers, a teapot. No wonder it was so heavy. Oh my god, Patricia, it's a treasure trove."

"You can take the silver if you like."

"No, Patricia, thanks. It's yours."

"I'm not using it and don't drink tea." She smiled. She was beginning to recover. I was not – she had given me a fright.

I was holding this soft paper wrap. "What on earth is . . .?" I unwrapped it cautiously.

"That's Eliot's hair, when she cut it. You can have that too."

"No, Patricia, thank you, but I'll put it back, with the silver."

The hair was tied with a string. It was a long braid, light brown, with a tinge, very faint, of red, actually, of gold. It was so soft, it felt "alive", and it made me sad. Tears were running down my face. I needed to blow my nose and couldn't find a tissue. So stupid, so embarrassing. I cleared the tears with a dusty hand.

I took out old newspapers that crumbled, disintegrating in my hands, quite a few dusty folders, and a bunch of loose sheets. The smell of dust, decay and mould had covered the fragrance of the "comfort soup" and was actually taking over the room, saturating the place. I thought I was getting sick. Perhaps I should better go to the bathroom, I thought.

Then, "Patricia, there are some manuscripts here," I said, my voice like a toad's croak.

Spellbound, I took the folders and the loose sheets – over the years some had been eaten up by bookworms – and put them, one after another, on the little table next to her.

We began to read.

"It's a collection of poems, *The Wild Heart*. Then there are other poems, wrapped in newspapers. . . . Pat, a big manuscript."

"What's the title on it? *Return to the Wilderness* . . . I don't know anything about it."

There was dust all over the floor, on my clothes, on the trunk, on the folders. My hands were black; my face must have been too. I had never felt so rewarded in my life. We had found our treasure.

Venice

May 2004

For years I had searched for details about Eliot Bliss's life, trying to understand *why* she had been forgotten, especially after the reprint of her two books. But even after meeting Patricia I had no satisfactory explanation. True, Eliot was poor. In the introduction to *Luminous Isle* she says she went into oblivion because she could not afford to go around, meet people and socialize, because she had no clothes to wear. Patricia confirmed they could barely survive on a single salary (Patricia's) – but was it a valid reason? She was poor and lesbian; had she been *rich* and lesbian, she could most probably continue to be part of the London literary circles.

I hoped the many letters and documents that I brought back with me would provide a clear answer. I knew I would have to try to contact Anna Wickham's family. Patricia had told me that Anna's son, George Hepburn, was still alive, so I had to plan another trip to England.

And I had to try to find out where exactly Ms Alexandra Pringle might be. My letters to Virago had never been answered. Patricia had told me Ms Pringle not only had the two books reprinted, but also she became Eliot's literary agent and friend.

To my disappointment, only a couple of folders were actually clean enough to be read and handled without the risk of permanent damage. The rest of the documents would have to be cleaned and disinfected with proper tools by a restorer, whom I couldn't afford. (Later, in 2006, my university would grant me the small sum needed for the cleaning and disinfection of the Eliot Bliss material.)

Back at home, hoping I had not transported with me a whole squadron of British bookworms, I dusted the letters and the manuscripts with care, and threw away old rusty clips, substituting them with plastic ones. Then I sorted the items, storing those that didn't show any sign of deterioration in a red box. The rest I put in blue boxes, filling a whole shelf in my studio.

She had mentioned *Return to the Wilderness* so many times in her 1960s and 1970s diaries, writing revision after revision. Luckily the carbon-copy manuscript Patricia and I had found was in almost perfect condition.

⠀⠀»⟫⟪«

In the spring of 2004 I began reading the contents of the red box. It contained a number of letters from the office of R. Cobden-Sanderson, Ltd, Publishers, in Maida Vale. Others were from Peter Davies, the publisher, praising Eliot for the collection of poems she had sent him, suggesting they should be published. He was probably referring to one of the collections in the red box, either *Selected Poems* or *The Wild Heart*. I created a small pile of letters from publishers, then sorted them by date and began reading.

One with an illegible signature made me jump. Patricia had never heard of the existence of a book called *The Albatross*, although she remembered many others that could not be found. The letter read:

> R. Cobden-Sanderson, Ltd.: Publishers
> 30th May 1935
> [. .]
>
> Dear Miss Bliss,
> We could wait until the end of July for "THE ALBATROSS" but we really cannot wait a moment later, if it is to come out this Autumn. I am longing to see the M.S., it sounds most promising.
> I am dreadfully sorry that you have been so ill. I can fully sympathise with you as I have been unwell myself, off and on, ever since the first of February.
> Yours ever sincerely,

The second letter had an attached note:

> R. Cobden-Sanderson, Ltd.: Publishers
> [. .]
> 20th June 1935
>
> Dear Miss Bliss,

Thank you ever so much. You have been most helpful. I send you the attached effort.

If you disapprove of it, will you let me know?

Yours ever sincerely,

The "attached effort" read:

From the publisher:

"THE ALBATROSS"

Miss Eliot Bliss's new novel represents an important departure both from her own earlier works and from the conventional modern novel. It is more objectively written than her previous book and while retaining points which made her "LUMINOUS ISLE" so generally admired, it has a new vividness, which makes her portrayal of the many characters who appear in its pages startlingly clear and incisive.

"THE ALBATROSS" is a series of impressions of London Nights, over a period of ten years while the city gradually changes. These impressions are seen through one mind and yet represent many minds or facets of the strange and varied city life. Every form and type of person drifts across its pages, each somehow, by however slender a thread, connected to the other, and yet most of them unaware of this central idea which binds them together. Some are famous, and some are not; the academician and the pavement artist, the statesman and the tub-thumper, all play their parts as units in the general scheme: and yet though so different, Miss Bliss has managed to depict one and all with a sensitiveness and an intimacy for which those who did not read "LUMINOUS ISLE" will find themselves quite unprepared.

Although the book is composed of many changing, swiftly moving, scenes, it lacks nothing in unity and every character, while complete in him or her self, is also contributory to the definite and central plan, which springs from the ordinary life of a great town.

Miss Bliss' many readers will find in "THE ALBATROSS" a more than worthy successor to "LUMINOUS ISLE".

Quickly I went through all the letters in the red box, but didn't find any further mention of *The Albatross*. Perhaps other letters or notes were among the blue boxes, the "possibly infected ones".

The book existed. Was it ever published? If it *was,* why could I not find any copy of it, and why could librarians not trace it anywhere? And if it *was not,* then why did the *Who Was Who* list it among Bliss's published works?

As I had already discovered, Cobden-Sanderson closed down in 1937, two years after the date of publication, and its archives whereabouts were unknown.

I called Patricia many times that spring, to check on her health and just to chat. When I told her about the letters from Cobden-Sanderson, she was thrilled but confirmed what she had told me already: that she had never heard of *The Albatross*.

If I wanted to find it, I had to look for the Cobden-Sanderson archives.

⫸⫷

"Do you think we can afford a week in England this summer as a vacation?" I asked my husband.

"Why England?" He turned his head and looked puzzled.

"Well, Alexander has never been to England. He'd love London, and I could work on my research while on vacation . . ."

"You mean you want to see Patricia Allan-Burns again."

"Well, she fascinates me. She is a good person. But it is not just that – though after reading the letters, the poems, and the manuscript of *Return to the Wilderness*, I have many questions to ask her. And then, I would also like to meet the Hepburns."

"Any university funds?" He enquired with a broad smile.

"You must be kidding."

⫸⫷

Before leaving, I got in touch with the British Library. Though my search through their online catalogue had failed to uncover anything of interest to me, I thought I might get lucky, and they would know something about *The Albatross* or Cobden-Sanderson.

From: Michela A. Calderaro
To: Modern-British@bl.uk
Subject: Eliot Bliss
Date: 4 July 2004

Dear Madam/Sir,
    I teach English and Postcolonial literature at the University of Trieste and

I'm writing a biography of writer Eliot (Eileen) Bliss. I have difficulties in finding out copyright owners and also to locate a novel she wrote, *The Albatross*, published by Cobden-Sanderson in 1935. I know this publisher closed down around 1937/39 but I cannot find out where their archive ended up.

Any help will be appreciated.

Best regards,

Michela Calderaro

Their answer was not what I had hoped for. Unfortunately, though they had searched the British Library's integrated catalogue and a number of other bibliographic sources, they had been able to trace neither *The Albatross* nor the rights-holder of Eliot Bliss's works. Their suggestion was to get in touch with Virago Press, who had recently reprinted two of her books. They provided me with an address, the one for Brettenham House, Lancaster Place, London, to which I had previously sent my inquiry.

CHAPTER 5

The War and Gardenia Cottage

Bishop's Stortford
7 July 2004

This time I did not wander around looking for the entrance. The apartment door was open, and I walked in.

Patricia seemed happy to see me, and I was relieved to observe that she was fine and looked well; she would turn ninety in a couple of months. I told her that the recording of our April conversations had not come out well. Actually, it was a disaster. So, would she mind going over a few episodes again, besides clarifying my many doubts about Eliot's work and life? Of course she wouldn't mind, she said. She was pleased to know that I would see the Hepburns the coming weekend.

We sat as we had in April and talked like old friends, about my son, whom she wanted to meet, and about her niece Harriet, Isobel's daughter, her niece Sue, Maeve's daughter, and how Maeve and Sue and her cousin from America, Sheila, would come visit her in August. She also told me about Lorna, the daughter of her best friend, Sally Bailey, who had died in an airplane crash when Lorna and her siblings were young. Two planes collided when the French controllers went on strike. She was flying back from Spain at the time. Lorna, now Mrs Lorna Zumpe, who used to work at the Coram Foundation for Children, in London, called her "Auntie Pat", and would take her to London, usually on her birthdays, to go to the opera, of which Patricia was very fond.

She then turned to a subject that had bothered her since April: what had happened to Eliot's manuscripts? And where could we find *The Albatross*? My search for Bliss had become *our* search.

Patricia had never interfered in Eliot's work. She had never read her manuscripts, never asked what she should do with her writings; she would only tie
the sheets with blue, or red silken ribbons. Now she regretted her discreetness.

"Maybe I should have interfered . . . asked her about the work, asked her
to read larger parts. She would give me a few pages, without telling me what
it was about, and I thought it was fine. It was her writing. It was her life . . ."

She stopped, looking pensive.

"I found another folder with poems, in her room," she went on. "It says
A Selection of Poems. And then many more pictures and letters, some in the
backroom; I want you to have that too."

"Are you sure? Patricia, you've given me a bundle already."

"Yes, I know you'll take good care of these things. You'll write about Eliot.
Her work is important. It was her life. . . . I'm still worried about what happened to *Hostile Country*. I can't understand it. And the play *Seti* – I got all the
books for her, some of them came from the London Library, and she worked
very hard. You know, she worked for a long time on this. I remember I would
tie the pages with nice ribbons."

"But it disappeared," I said. "Maybe she gave the manuscripts to someone,
because they were ready for publication. What I understood from her diaries
is that she had completed the manuscripts of *Hostile Country* and *Seti* and was
very pleased with them."

"Yes, one wonders what happened."

"If somebody had taken it up, they would have done something with it, but
they didn't. Even what you gave me, the one we found in the trunk, *Return
to the Wilderness*, is only a carbon copy. Which means the original must be
somewhere."

"It is strange, isn't it? I don't understand. All her work . . ."

"If I can find some publisher willing to publish Eliot's work, would you . . .?"

"Oh, dear, she wished so much to have her books published. Yes, of course.
What do you want to know, dear? That's the main thing."

"Just talk, Patricia. I'll ask you questions if there's something I don't understand. Also, if you can tell me again about you and the 1930s, and how you
came to be . . . here."

She began:

"I was born in Chapman. I had been a pupil at the art school, and I got a scholarship to go to the Central School of Arts and Crafts on Southampton Row. I got a grant as well, but my father would only let me go if I stayed with, you know. . . . My sister Isobel was living in London at the time, but she couldn't put me up. Patience and Eliot were able to put me up in 1A Hill Side Road, St John's Wood. And Patience Ross – how do I put it? – I told you about Eliot and Marty. And, well, I presume that Patience then fell in love with Louise Hoyt Porter,[1] an American, and they sort of went off together. Then Eliot and I were alone.

"And we had various flats in London. We had one on Elmwood Road, then on Clifton Road, and the last one was on Warwick Avenue, which was very near to Clifton Road. A fellow student at the Central School, Paul Beadle[2] – he was a beautiful draftsman, he also sculptured the head that you see there." She was pointing at a beautiful child's head, on a shelf in a corner, near the bay window. "He had to leave London [during the war] because they had some bomb damage. He wrote and said, 'If anything happens, you just pack and come down to Gardenia Cottage, Spellbrook'. Well, something *did* happen, and we came down to Bishop's Stortford, where he said to get a taxi out to Gardenia Cottage. And it was sort of twilight. . . . Oh, dear."

She coughed, then continued. "I remember we arrived at Gardenia Cottage. It was bang on the main road. Eliot said, *This can't be it!* Oh, dear, but it *was* it, a cottage with a dirt floor and two rooms upstairs. No water, no drain, no

---

1   According to a post on Fiona Richards's site, Patience Ross and Louise Hoyt Porter moved to West Sussex, and Patience, referred to as Miss Ropes, "died [there] around 1988, having developed dementia". *John Ireland: Music, People, Places*, https://johnirelandmusicpeopleplaces.wordpress.com/2014/04/28/irelands-books-patience-ross/comment-page-1/#comment-235.

2   Michael Dunn, "Figurative Sculpture Post-1960", chapter 7 in *New Zealand Sculpture: A History* (Auckland: Auckland University Press, 2008), 86–90. "Among the most prominent sculptors to emerge in these years [the 1960s] was Paul Beadle (1917–1992). Born and trained in Britain, he had spent the years from 1944 to 1960 in Australia before shifting to Auckland. Bohemian in type, Beadle was a large bearded figure whose shorts and sandals became something of a trademark. His contribution to the visual arts as a practitioner, administrator and spokesperson was wide in scope and impact and his genial personality helped establish him quickly in his new environment. There his work underwent rapid change and evolution. . . . At the outbreak of war, Beadle joined the Royal Navy, serving in the Home Mediterranean and Pacific fleets. He served as submariner and in that capacity went to Australia in 1944. At war's end, having no desire to go back to England, he turned to teaching art."

light. We lived there for . . . must have been seven years, because we came into Bishop's Stortford in 1948. My firm – you know I worked there as an industrial engraver – had been allocated some prefabricated bungalows, and I was offered one of them, and that's how we came to be in Bishop's Stortford: 15 Firlands, Bishop's Stortford.

"You could imagine," she went on. "You hear 'Gardenia Cottage at Spellbrook', and you imagine a lovely cottage, roses around the door. And we ended up on . . . I mean, the path was literally about *that* wide, and that was the main London road. Anyway it was somewhere to be. It was home.

"Reading Paul Beadle's letter, you could not imagine how terrible the place was. He had got a cottage with his girlfriend, Lily, in Ashton, and then he went to the Navy. He was in a submarine, and when the war ended, the submarine was in Australian waters. I've never seen him again. He was demobbed there, and he chose to stay in Australia. He was a great fine sculptor.

"One evening, during the war, he and Lily came to have supper with us in Warwick Avenue, and there were pubs and shops across the street, and so Paul wanted to go and have a drink. I didn't go, but he, Eliot and Lily went. Then he came back and said, 'I'm not going to spend here another night', because shrapnel had been falling while they were in the pub. He said, 'No, I shall not be coming again.' They went back to where they lived, and then he was gone. And then, of course, he wrote to us from Spellbrook saying, 'If anything happens to you, come here.'

"Shrapnel were falling, dear, oh dear. Yes, 'cause you see, during the war, what one had to do . . . We used to make a large pot of coffee and some sandwiches, and go down to the cellar of the house, and stay there. And then when there was the all-clear signal, we would walk in the street. There was always an awful smell of bricks and rubber, not very pleasant.

"And then, of course, moving from Warwick Avenue to Gardenia Cottage. . . . You had to walk across the main road, across and up the lane to where there was a pump for the water, carry buckets. We had two white tin enamelled pails. Pippa, our cat, would not come up that lane, would not go any further. I collected the water from the pump. And we also had oil lamps . . ."

"How would you cook?"

"We had an open great firelight, and next to it there was an oven, and on this side you put the water, which was heated by the fire. And you cooked in the oven, and you had something where you put a saucepan on. In the summer we had a sort of primer stove, and we had a little shade in the garden."

"How was the neighbourhood?"

"There were three other cottages and the Greyhound Pub, all on the main road, and next on this side there was a sort of garage. It belonged to a Mr Chapman, and then there was Mr Whitman, the baker, who always kept the water pump well legged. It always worked. He was a very nice man, Mr Whitman. He believed in homemade wine. He made his own wine. He would say, 'Have a glass of this every day, my dear.'

"Then you went a little bit uphill, where there were some houses, and down here more houses. So there were these four cottages. They had started to demolish them . . . and everybody used to go to the pub, and there was the – what you call – the public bar, and then there was the corridor, and then sort of another bar. Eliot and I used to stand in this corridor.

"And then, of course, when Eliot suffered severe bronchitis we met Dr Burton, who became a friend forever. He was a wonderful doctor. He was a very good doctor, I must say. In Spellbrook, Eliot had these very bad bouts of bronchitis. He used to come any time of the day. He would be on his way, and would come to see how she was.

"He really cared. And he pulled her through. And then, you see, what happened was I became of an age when I would be called for war work. I was supposed to go to a factory in Birmingham, and Dr Burton intervened and said that Eliot could not be left alone, so I was exempted. And we had to go to a medical tribunal. Not funny. So that's how I came to work at Prior's.

"Originally they were making microscopes, but they turned and everything they did was for gun sighting. So that was my war work, really."

So that's what happened – the war had brought them here.

"It is understandable that later on she would get sick, but when you met her . . .?" I asked.

"She was better in London, but was very ill in Spellbrook. And then we came to Bishop's. It was incredible to turn the light switch and turn the tap for water. We moved with the cats to the aluminium buildings in Bishop's Stortford in 1948.

"We always had cats. They were very good company, also in wartime. The last two lovely ones we had, they used to sleep on her bed. They were on her bed always. It was wonderful. And in London, during the war, people would say to watch the cats, and it was true. If the building was going to be bombed, the cats would leave before. They must have some extrasensory perception. It was true, though people laughed at me when I told them."

"The aluminium buildings, were they all furnished, with everything?"

"Oh, yes. The kitchen was equipped with everything, and they had built cabinets. They came in pieces fitted together. Later on Eliot loathed to leave it!

"Prior's allocated twenty aluminium buildings for their so-called skilled workers, and I got one. That was the only reason. I couldn't have got a house, or anything, you know.

"She was often in bed, and her hands had got swollen extraordinarily. But she did, she did recover. Though later on she also got arthritis. But we were already in Bishop's Stortford, and it was 1953, and thereafter she was never well. I think [because] she had menopause, you know. Ladies change in life. She had terrible migraines."

"In her diaries, she mentions her bad health. She keeps writing about not feeling well."

"She wasn't well. Terrible migraines. She wasn't well for some considerable time. She had, as I told you, these egg-shaped swellings on her hands and legs. And then Dr Lee, who was our doctor then, sent her to the hospital. Within forty-eight hours she had it all over her. It was incredible, it was dreadful. I was able to go, after work, and you couldn't believe it. It was absolutely . . . it was all over.

"She was in the hospital for six months. In those days they gave gold injections. She had a terrible amount of physiotherapy. They put her in a sort of coffin-bed with lights, lamps. She was in Barnard Ward, which is a medical ward, and she made friends with a lot of patients, who were also there, and was in correspondence with them when she came out.

"But she had gone in quite a well-built person and came out a skeleton. Arthritis, it burns you. It is extraordinary. She came home, because she thought she was going to die and she wanted to die at home, so . . .

"Fortunately, we had a very good neighbour, Mrs Radcliffe. She was great help – I still hear from her – she was wonderful, because I had to work . . . I couldn't. . . . I used to go into her bedroom at about three, four in the morning, and she'd been wet through, absolutely wet through. Even her head was wet. It was incredible. And I used to wash her, 'cause she had to go to bed in these plasters. Her legs had to be put in these plasters. And I used to get up, wash her and . . . I couldn't dress her, but she used to have a housecoat, and I'd get her into a chair in the sitting room, and Mrs Radcliffe used to pop in and out while I was at work, and she used to get some lunch ready, so I gave her lunch when I came home at lunchtime.

"I used to wrap her wrists with long white silken ribbons to hide the swelling, especially when she would go up to London. She didn't want people to . . ."

She closed her eyes, I let her rest.

After a while she stood up, and went to make coffee, then she was back to her armchair, ready to continue to talk about Eliot's works. "So, dear, tell me, what do you make of her manuscript?"

"Patricia, I think she based *Return to the Wilderness* on the experience in Spellbrook, and the later move to Bishop's Stortford. She changed the names, but she is certainly drawing from her own life: she changed the name of the cottage into Magnolia Cottage."

"Is it any good?"

"It is *very* autobiographical!" I replied with a smile and began reading the first pages.

She listened, as if transported back in time.

> In the April of nineteen forty-eight, the third year of the peace, my life started to change. After seven years spent in what I always thought of as exile – in a small village on the border of Essex in an unprepossessing, even ugly countryside, we moved house. This house moving was symptomatic of the change beginning to take place in the country as a whole, as well as in my whole life. For the new place we were moving to was an estate being built under a Government Housing Scheme three miles away in the neighbouring market town, and Fay Clancy, my second cousin, and I were allotted a house on it. We had had an old roomy Victorian flat in London for some years till bombs drove us out, and we had almost by accident come to live in a small labourer's cottage which a sculptor friend, called up from the Navy, had passed on to us and which he had christened before going – "Magnolia Cottage" – to the surprise of the villagers who had always known of it as No. 1 "King's Head" Cottages.
>
> The cottage, before its brief tenancy, had been condemned and had also been falling to pieces, but was bought and done up by an eccentric Quaker landlord – also fleeing from bombs – who had let it to the sculptor and then

to us. "Magnolia Cottage" was one of those ancient dwellings which can only be patched up, and after seven years it was again in need of repairs and was again bought by someone from London – this time for six times its original price – and we would have had to have gone even if we had not had the offer of the new house on the housing estate.

Strangely enough, when the new house was ready and all the arrangements for the move, much as I thought I had hated the village, I felt quite passionately against leaving it. I had strong apprehension about the place we were moving to – the nearest large town of Abbot Abortford – (nor were these unfounded), and in spite of its many drawbacks, its lack of any ordinary amenities and its general primitiveness, I had become deeply attached to "Magnolia".

It had become our home – even in a special way – because we had not chosen it, but had been forced to live in it owing to the circumstances of war. It now held the atmosphere we had created. (*Return to the Wilderness*, part 1, End of Twilight, 1–2)

"So, from London to Spellbrook, because of the war."

"Yes, the place where we were before, on Warwick Avenue, the last place we had in London, was quite different, you know. I remember when the war was declared . . . Eliot used to sleep quite late at night and I was up and I was sitting – it was a sort of conservative place – and I remember a record being played, one was Alfred Cortot playing and another was Jean Sablon singing, then silence, and then came the news that we were at war. Oh yes, on the radio . . . Fifteen minutes later the air siren went off."

"I remember distinctly the music and the voice: 'We are now at war with Germany'. I had no idea then what it was going to be like. No."

The wind started to blow through the chimney. The lamenting sound had a chilling effect while she was recalling that moment in September 1939.

"Yes, it is the chimney," she explained.

"Are you tired?"

"I keep on wishing . . . I wish . . . she had a happier life. I don't like to think about it, because, you know, I so wish she'd been able to fulfil . . . I mean, to have so much potential and not being able to fulfil it."

"But you were here with her. Otherwise she would have been by herself."

"She should have been in her dear home."

"By herself!"

"She could have had a happier life. Her brain was flaming. I feel I failed her by not seeing that she . . . The war disrupted everything. Her Naval friends were all called for duty. There were three; the "pilot" was on duty at Portsmouth and was killed there. John, who went down in the wood . . . Charles. . . . All gone."

CAIRN

"We used to have in those days a service called *home care*, and we had someone coming for two hours, and that's when I would go out to town, you know, to work. So we had a lovely one who was with us for years. Mrs Smith. She was really good with Eliot, you know, very good with her. So I used to take my holiday when she had her holiday, because it would have been difficult. . . . Because Mrs Smith understood her so well. She was with us for years.

"It would have been difficult for her to have a strange person for two weeks. So I used to take my holiday from the firm in those two weeks."

"This was . . .?"

"After Sylvia's death."

Again she was lost in her reveries about Eliot, feeling guilty about the isolation and solitude into which she felt she had dragged Eliot. It was not the right moment to enquire about Sylvia.

"Patricia, it was also *your* life, and you devoted it to her."

"I don't know . . ."

After having our soup, I insisted Patricia take some rest. Our session had been extremely taxing for her, and when we resumed talking, late in the afternoon, I tried to introduce a lighter subject, one that would not evoke unpleasant memories.

"I remember you told me a beautiful story about a haunted house you lived in before moving to Gardenia Cottage."

"That was on Clifton Road. Our doctor had the ground floor, front and basement, and we had the middle floor, and there was a French professor and his wife on the top. That's where Cairn visited us. Well, the doctor left and moved to a house on Warwick Avenue, and the French professor and his wife left too, and we were left alone, and there was an awful noise up on the top floor. We even called the police, but nothing was found. In this flat we had two bedrooms and a sitting room, and you went downstairs to the kitchen and bathroom, and when I would go down to the bathroom and come back, Eliot would say, 'What did you go back upstairs for?' And, of course, I hadn't been upstairs, you know. It was like people rattling chains across the floor. Anyway, the doctor eventually told us they had [had] the same experience, haunting experience, but they didn't tell us anything [earlier], because they knew we were on our own.

"And so that was the time when Eliot went to America, and I'd seen her off at the boat train and came back to Clifton Road. Because I had to wait, we had a cat there, and the vet was going to come. A lady vet, who was going to collect the cat, because I had to move out of the apartment and into a bedsitting room, and also I had my luggage there. The cat's fur was all like . . . you know. A very peculiar feeling. We were alone in the flat, and she must have felt something."

"This was the first time Eliot went to America?"

Patricia stood up and went to the little desk, where she picked up a small parcel.

"I found these *things*, and I think you should have them. Letters, from Cairn. I recognized her handwriting. Clifton Road is where Cairn visited us. This Baker Quinn, we all called her Quinn, was in Spain, travelling with Cairn, and she wrote Eliot asking if we could put up Cairn. And Cairn arrived in Clifton Gardens and . . . they fell in love."[3]

Well, my wish to introduce a lighter subject had failed miserably. Cairn's story would turn out to be far from light.

"What was Cairn doing, also writing?"

"That time they were just travelling, like most Americans, just travelling. Cairn, I think she must have had some private income from her father, who lived in Florida. Ruth Stickney was her official name. Her mother later married Mr Howe. The second time Eliot went to America, Cairn had passed the exam to be an estate agent, so she was doing that. But what she was doing the first time, that I don't know. I don't think she had any job.

"Eliot kept her letters. I do recognize Cairn's handwriting, so those are

3   Baker Quinn had begun a correspondence with Eliot Bliss following the publication of *Saraband* in the United States in 1931, by sending a few clippings with reviews of the book.

the letters from Cairn. . . . In those days, of course, it was still the big trip, the big Atlantic boat."

"And the second time she went to America?"

"The Irving, 308 West Thirtieth, New York, a women's club, that's where she was staying until they started on that trip they were going. That was the time when things went badly, and I had to find the money for her to come back home. What happened I don't know, but obviously things went bad.[4] They didn't work out, 'cause I know when she came back, she said. . . . She was in the Los Angeles area. There were lots of Japanese people who were very kind to her. But, of course, she always drank, you know, and probably too much. But I don't know what happened. But anyway, Cairn still remained friends; during the war she sent us parcels, hidden always there would be cigarettes, yes, food parcels from America.

"I've still got the telegram that her mother sent to say that she died. She was going to be buried in Crosscreek Cemetery. I think it is in New York. I don't know if it is the Service's, 'cause she was in the Service during the war. So she might be buried in the Service's cemetery. I don't know, but I remember we had this telegram. Mrs Howe, her mother, wrote she had cancer.

"Eliot was very fond of Cairn. She used to come over, you see, when we were living in Firlands. She came over, yes."

Patricia sounded sad, and very tired.

"I think it was 1937 – you'll probably find out in the letters between Eliot and Cairn. I'm not at all sure, 'cause I was still going to school. It might have been earlier than that. It might have been the second time. She might have gone in '35. The first time she went. I spent my summer holiday with my parents in Wellington.

"We were still packing while going in the taxi to the boat train, 'cause she always took her pillows, whenever she went, wrapped up in rugs, rugs with some leather straps, and we were still packing in the taxi. Yes, I remember." She was laughing softly. "Dear, oh dear. That was her first trip to America. From Southampton."

"Where were you staying when she came back?"

---

4   It was impossible to find out what exactly happened during this second visit. Eliot had made friends there and had kept a close correspondence with some of Cairn's friends, especially with Louise Savage, who, like Cairn, lived in Connecticut.

"While she was in America, I stayed in a bedsitting room. But she said she was coming, that she'd be back for quite some time. So I found a place in Douglas Road, Canonbury, which in those days was a rather *down* area and is now most fashionable. But in those days it wasn't. I liked it. It was by the canal. And it had one room and a kitchen, quite a large kitchen, and you had a bath downstairs. And that was where she came back to when she returned form America. She wouldn't have stayed at a YWCA."

When Eliot went to America the second time, she left Patricia in the care of two gay friends.

"Very nice people – they were told to look after me!"

"So you were still in school."

"Yes, I was still at Central School, I've never finished school – when she came back we were so close to war. In my summer break from school I used to work in a shop, a garments and hats shop. We had some lovely customers. There was a judge's wife. . . . She used to ask me to try on her outfits for Ascot, 'cause we had the same build! It was fun. Clothes and hats!"

"And then you moved to . . ."

"Warwick Avenue, which is actually very near to Clifton Road, where we had been. Warwick Avenue in those days was like a small village, you know. You had shops and pubs where everybody used to go. It is quite different now, but in those days quite like a small village, rather nice. And then, of course, we came down to Gardenia Cottage. As I told you, when we came down to Gardenia Cottage – two women on their own – the people in the village thought of us . . . uh, well, they thought we were ladies of the night. But by the time we left, they were great friends. It was so amusing. Ladies of the night. So funny."

"Well, you came down from London and were different from the villagers."

The doorbell startled us, both of us lost in the past as we were.

"Qui est là?" she asked in French.

"Qui est là?" I repeated, smiling.

I walked to the door and let in a man.

"Mrs Burns?" he called out.

"Oh, the people from the library," Patricia said and stood up. "Thank you very much," she said to him. "Here, these books are to be taken." She was pointing at a pile of books on a stool.

I went back to the studio. Looking out, I could see the library van, which provided a weekly book-lending service to people who could not reach the library on their own.

She followed the man and started for the door.

"Could I do anything?" I asked her.

"You stay right here and be comfortable."

"Is it raining? You better . . ."

"No, no." She went out with the man, who was carrying the books, and they headed to the library van.

The music played on, softly.

※※※

Later on, I was able to find some information about Cairn's mother:

> Sammie Howe (March 7, 1887–September 12, 1999) was an American verified supercentenarian. She was born in Greenville, Alabama. She married young (aged sixteen) to Percy Stickney. They had a daughter called Ruth.
>
> In 1912, the family travelled to Paris, France. On the way back home, they were part of the ship SS *Carpathia*, which rescued passengers that survived the *Titanic* disaster. Howe later divorced and remarried – this time to a banker from Florida. Howe was a fan of the basketball team Orlando Magic.
>
> Howe died on March 7, 1999, at the age of 112 years, 189 days.[5]

More could be found in an *Orlando Sentinel* obituary:

> Sammie Howe, 112, Was Among Oldest in Florida
>
> Sammie Howe outlived a century and most of her family. But she didn't outlive her memories of times gone by.
>
> Howe of Orlando, who celebrated her 112th birthday in March, died Sunday. She was thought to be one of Florida's oldest residents.
>
> Until she went into a nursing home 12 years ago, Howe lived at Lucerne Towers, a retirement home, for about 10 years.
>
> There, Howe met Marguerite Jones, who became her dearest friend and, eventually, her caretaker.

---

5   "Sammie Howe," Gerontology Wiki, http://gerontology.wikia.com/wiki/Sammie _Howe.

The two women, both widows, spent hours feeding the pigeons and squirrels outside their high-rise and trading memories, said Jones, a Lucerne Towers resident for 20 years.

"Sammie said she was on the ship that picked up the survivors of the *Titanic*," said Jones, 93.

"She and her husband and daughter were returning from a trip to Paris.

"She said [her] ship's crew handed her a baby from the *Titanic* and she cared for it until they arrived in New York."

Howe's ship, the SS *Carpathia*, owned by the Cunard Line, rescued about 700 Titanic passengers about two hours after the celebrated ship sank, taking with it more than 1,500 people, in 1912.

The baby Howe cared for, Jones said, was claimed by the child's grandfather in New York. The parents perished at sea.

A native of Greenville, Ala., Howe married twice and had one child, Ruth, who died at age 54.

Howe was just 16 when she married Ruth's father, Percy Stickney, the son of a wealthy Jacksonville family, Jones said.

The Howes traveled extensively in Europe. Two years after the sinking of the *Titanic*, Sammie Howe volunteered to drive for an American general while vacationing in Paris during World War I, Jones said.

The Howes' marriage eventually ended in divorce. She later married a Florida banker and settled in Pine Castle, south of Orlando. After his death, Howe moved briefly to New York City to be near a nephew, who also died.

She returned to Orlando in the early 1970s, Jones said.

"I loved her dearly and took good care of her," said Jones, who handled Howe's move to a nursing home when she broke her hip.

"I was the only person in the world she had."

September 15, 1999.

Sandra Mathers of *The Sentinel* Staff[6]

SYLVIA

"Eliot was not happy here. She had only few friends. There was Dr Burton's son, George – he was a great person, because he used to come and stay in the

---

6 Sandra Mathers, "Sammie Howe, 112, Was Among Oldest in Florida", *Orlando Sentinel*, 15 September 1999, http://articles.orlandosentinel.com/1999-09-15/news/9909140426_1_howe -titanic-jones.

flat. We had a wheelchair which was lent to us by the Congregational Church, and we used to take her out to a pub nearby, in Firlands, on the other side of town from here. I don't recall how the pub was called . . . Anyway, you can go and see. I always remember George. He used to *race* the wheelchair. But he was awfully good, because he was company for her.

"Unfortunately he is gone, you know. He had an M.C. [Military Cross][7] from the war. He served, dear George. He was great company to her. He was great, George, he really was. 'Cause you know, they could talk books and things, everything in life they would talk about.

"He had a bad period when he came back from the war. Eliot said he should have gone to university. That was really what he wanted, an academic life. Eliot was very fond of him. He used to come and stay at Firlands. He used to sleep on the sofa that we had there. [. . .] He would make his own breakfast and then take Eliot to the pub with the wheelchair, then race back. I'll never forget him racing back with the wheelchair. They had built a ramp. We had a front door and a back door, but the back door had steps, so the council built a ramp.

"They kept in touch. I know that George felt that my brain wasn't academic enough for Eliot – which is true, quite true. I hadn't had the background or the education that Eliot had. I wasn't intellectual enough for her."

She paused for a long, long time. I didn't know what to say, so I thought it better to go back to Eliot's diaries.

"On the list that Eliot herself had prepared, with names and initials of people she used to know, there was a John Williams. His name appears many times in her diaries. She wrote he would visit, and he was also at Sylvia's funeral."

"John Williams was a dear friend. Actually, I met him when I was working at the Boar's Head, and we became friends. He worked in London, but lived in Bishop's. He used to come and bring a bottle of wine. He was at Eliot's funeral. And then, yes, the other great thing was when Sylvia came."

---

7   "Medals: Campaigns, Descriptions and Eligibility", https://www.gov.uk/medals-campaigns-descriptions-and-eligibility.
   Instituted in 1914, the M.C., Military Cross, was "awarded to all ranks of the RN, RM, Army, and RAF in recognition of exemplary gallantry during active operations against the enemy on land. An ornamental cross in silver, with straight arms terminating in broad finals ornamented with Imperial Crowns. At the centre on the cross is the Royal Cypher (King George VI shown here). The reverse of the cross is plain in design, though at certain times the year of the award has been engraved."

"Sylvia . . ." At last.

"Eliot had known Sylvia in the years of Anna Wickham, and she ran into her one day, at the Fitzroy. She told Eliot she'd been living in a bed-sitting room, and they had been afar. So Eliot said, 'Put your things on a carrier bag, get on a train and come down'. Which she did. And then – *there* was Sylvia, you know. And she stayed . . .

"I'll take a look at the soup, dear."

"Do you need any help?"

"No, dear."

◄◄◄ ►►►

Later, over soup, she went on, but not directly about Sylvia.

"Eliot didn't want to come here. The bungalow where we were living in Firlands was very nice. It had a garden, and you get used to it. And moves are not easy at all.

"She didn't like Bishop's Stortford anyway. Well, it wasn't her world, dear. She preferred Firlands. She liked it. She should never have lived here. I mean she should have been in London with her like-minded people.

"She was very fond of John Heath-Stubs, the poet. They used to have telephone conversations. He's still alive, I think. He's a very good poet. . . . She was very fond of him.

"And then there was John Gawsworth. Jim Hepburn brought Odie Smith down to see her here. He was Olivia Manning's husband. These are the people she should have been living among. There was nothing for her here, just . . . you know."

"But here you could take care of her," I reasoned. "She was so sick."

"Oh, yes, I know that, dear. But if she had been in London, a lot of people would come and see her, whereas to come here is a journey. If she had been in London, if *we* had been in London, I would have looked after her, people would come to visit, and she wouldn't have felt so out of everything. No, she should never have been here."

Finishing her soup, she leaned back. "London. There's no place like London, really. And here. . . . The only happy times she had here were when Sylvia was here. Sylvia came when we were living in Firlands, and they used to have half,

94

or a whole, bottle of wine. Sylvia – she knew the same world, Sylvia. Those were the happiest times."

"In the diaries there's a loose note, a letter written by George Hepburn and sent from Brighton to Eliot at the Royal Hotel, Woburn Place, London. Eliot was hoping to meet him there, and he mentioned the fact that Sylvia in that period had left Firlands. He writes, 'I don't think that Sylvia would come back', and also that Eliot had injured herself, or something to that effect. The letter reads,

> 17 May 1959
>
> My Dear Eliot,
> Thank you for your letter – and for the invitations, neither of which, alas, I can accept. I'm too broke.
> I hope you enjoy your stay in London – the theatres etc., and hope Sylvia is sufficiently recovered to come and meet you. I wonder still, whether she will ever return to you in B. Stortford.
> Sorry about the fall, but hope all is well now.

"I think she went twice back to London, but she couldn't manage," said Patricia. "It became too difficult. Because during the war Sylvia had been trapped in a building – I don't know where it was. And she said the only friend she had was a rat. *He* sort of stayed with her. Over that period I think she semi-starved, because, when she came to Bishop's Stortford, our doctor, who attended to her, told me that what happened was that she had been through a period of starvation which had eaten her muscles. She was terribly thin, and always cold. And he explained that no matter what, she would never put on any weight because of this period that she'd gone through, you know.

"She had the most beautiful voice, Sylvia. She was terribly thin, and she used to have a chair by the fire, always cold."

"Was she dark, or blonde?"

"She was grey, dear. When I knew her she was grey. She was a great beauty in her days.

She had quite a few affairs, and she was involved in a murder trial. I think a man killed someone for her. I don't recall exactly. Augustus John was one of her lovers, dear, oh dear. There, you see, in her youth she had lived in what is called *society*, that of John Kirkwood. And she was a great friend of Lady

Louise Mountbatten, and lived in that circle. She had, in her youth. And that's where her friendship with John Kirkwood came from, 'cause he'd known her already from those years. It was through Anna. It was that sort of circle. She had a really beautiful voice, speaking voice. Wheeler Williams,[8] the sculptor, was one of her husbands. He used to send her money when she was with us.

"During the time Sylvia was here, Eliot was happier. She had a degree of happiness because she had companionship. They read books and poems. Sylvia had known them all, you know. And, yes, it was wonderful for her.

"Unfortunately, she died. Eliot was in the room behind, where you've been before; Sylvia was in the back, the backroom. She fell down and broke her femur, and it was at night. We had to get an ambulance, and she was taken to the hospital and . . . she died.

"I think it was too much. I went up to visit her, you know. Poor Sylvia. She was seventy-eight. She had always wanted to live to be eighty. Poor Sylvia, she didn't manage. . . . Do you mind if I have a cigarette, now?"

"Of course not! But your asthma . . ."

She smiled as if to make me understand that asthma was just another thing she was putting up with.

"Please put that down in the kitchen, dear."

I collected the dishes and carried them to the kitchen. When I came back, she was lost in her memories. She was back to Eliot's trips to America.

"I'm sorry I can't be of more help. I don't remember when she went to America. I just remember all the packing. Dear, oh dear. She had this special, little pillow, about *this* size . . ."

"That she would carry with her, like you told me."

"She slept with it. But she also took other pillows. I always remember this packing . . . Oh dear, it is still there, on the armchair, next to the fireplace, behind you."

There it was, the tiny pillow she had always carried with her; whitish, no pattern, in fine soft cotton. I felt so sad.

⊱⊰

---

8   Wheeler Williams (30 November 1897–12 August 1972) was an American sculptor, born in Chicago, Illinois.

"Fifteen Firlands. It's where Sylvia joined us, you see. We were living in Firlands when it happened. When Eliot had told her to put her things on a carrier bag, get on a train and come, she did, and stayed till the end of her life.

"Sylvia did go back to London, I don't remember if it was once or twice, but she couldn't manage to stay away. She loved London, and liked to drink at the Fitzroy. That was her. . . . But she was no longer able to look after herself. Sylvia had come to that. She had, really. She couldn't. Dear Sylvia. And all the years Sylvia was with us, she was great company for Eliot. It made a great difference, and Eliot had the company she wanted. Sylvia was very intelligent, very well read. They knew the *world*. They used to have a little hot bottle of Spanish wine for lunch, you know."

For a while there was only silence.

"After Sylvia died, Eliot would take short trips to London; she used to stay in a hotel, usually the County Hotel, in Russell Square, and John Kirkwood would look after her. Good John, he was wonderful. A kind person. He arranged everything for her comfort, you know. He took her out. He'd arrange it, also because of her condition, with two sticks. He arranged everything. He was that kind of person, and I always knew she was going to be looked after. They used to make appointments with George [George Hepburn]. She was very fond of George. I haven't seen George for a long time, but he was beautiful, George. Oh, yes, he really was. We only speak on the telephone now, only occasionally, I'm afraid."

The wind was shaking the branches outside the window. She lit another cigarette.

"After Sylvia's death, Eliot kept writing how worried she was about Sylvia's son," I said.

"Oh, when the son appeared at the Crematorium . . . God! I couldn't believe it. Extraordinary! 'Cause, I mean, really, Eliot couldn't go to the funeral. John Kirkwood came with me, and then the son appeared. Dear, oh dear. A peculiar piece of life. She had two sons. One died, and we knew there was one left. She always spoke of her boys. They both went to Eton, I think, from the way she used to speak. Even John Kirkwood had tried to get in touch with him, so that he could visit his mother. 'Cause he thought he had to do something; she was not a healthy woman. We looked at a list of the Gough family, but she was not mentioned. As far as I understood, Sylvia was loved by many men, and then there was the murder, and the trial, and it didn't go well with the Gough family, 'cause, of course, it was all over the newspapers.

"John tried in various London clubs which he thought [the son] might belong to. But he didn't reply. What happened was we had a note put up in the *Daily Telegraph* and the *Times* about Sylvia's death – that's how he must have learnt about it. George Gough must still be alive. I was trying to think, when he arrived at the funeral, how old did he look – late forties, I would say. He might still be alive.

"Sylvia was a lovely person, she may have been gay in her youth, but so was John Kirkwood; they lived a sort of very privileged life. . . . I don't know when she married, she was seventy-eight when she died. Well, say the son was in his late forties, he must have been born when she was in her thirties, so she probably married in her twenties. . . . Shall we have a glass of wine?"

A moment later, sipping my wine, I went on. "In her diaries, Eliot wrote a lot about John Kirkwood. Was he living in London? Is he still alive?"

"He died, dear. It was very sad, because I think he had brain tumour. What happened was he became ill, and he went to stay with his brother, in Sandwich; I can't remember, I think he is a *Sir*. John's mother had been a Tate, of Tate and Low. They had a nurse for him, but unfortunately . . . They looked after him until he died. And I think he was buried in the church, in Sandwich. I don't know if he was cremated, but he's got some *remembrance*, you know. Because Eliot used to speak to them on the telephone. They seemed to be very nice. They looked after John, for which one was very grateful, 'cause he had been such a lovely person. He was so good. He did give some financial help. He would, I know. Eliot said he contributed to the electric bill, and you know, I don't know how much, but I think on occasions he did. And he used to come down, which was nice."

The wind kept rustling the garden leaves outside. She lit another cigarette. She looked worn out, and melancholic.

"Shall I let you rest now?" I said. "I'll come back tomorrow, in the afternoon, and we'll talk."

"Yes, dear. I'll listen to the radio now. See you tomorrow."

◄◄►►

I was also tired. It had been a long day, and I felt exhausted, drained. I did not know where all this was taking me. Eliot had died fourteen years earlier. With these recollections, I was bringing back Pat's pain. I could feel it on my own skin, in waves. And it was not just the pain of Eliot's death.

They had led a solitary life, confined, in the countryside. Bishop's Stortford is, today, a big centre. Stansted Airport has brought work and prosperity to an otherwise uninteresting small village. Back then it had few things to offer Eliot, who would always complain about the place and its inhabitants – all the terrible stories she reported in her diaries. *I have never read the diaries*, Patricia had said. Well, perhaps it was better she didn't.

⟫⟪

8 July 2004

We were sipping coffee, black and *very* hot. I tried to resume the conversation where we had left it the day before: Sylvia the mystery woman. Patricia seemed tired, and I decided I wouldn't stay long.

"When we met in April, you mentioned that when Sylvia came over, you had to find an extra job."

"Oh, yes. If you go down into town, there is a corner exchange, what they call a C.E., and when you walk down Windhill there's a pub, the Boar's Head, where Samuel Pepys's diaries were written; he looked out from the Boar's Head, and that's where I worked. I used to walk from Firlands through the churchyard. I worked there Thursday night, Saturday morning and Saturday night and Sunday. Thursday is market day in Bishop's, and there were all the farmers, you know, so they needed help on Thursday night and Saturday."

"That's a lot of work!"

"Well, you know, you get used to work, dear, yes."

"But you were already working in the factory!" I couldn't help myself interfering, even though I had sworn I wouldn't.

"Yes, but you must get on with it, dear. I imagine there must have been times it was stressful, yes. That's how our life was. I could never understand Dr Lee regarding this point; because Eliot should have been able, in my opinion – due to all the years she had been infirm – she should have been entitled to some sort of pension. Well, Eliot had never worked, you know . . . I mean she worked in London at Crosby Hall, and she used to do examination papers. She even worked as a garage mechanic! And as a chauffeur for Nigel Playfair. But she never paid any stamps. I think she should have been entitled due to her illness, to some kind of social pension. It wasn't until we had been here some years and she was ill and we had another doctor, and he arranged for her to have . . . whatever it was. I never could understand Dr Lee. Well, it wasn't a great deal, but it was something."

"Between the factory, the Boar's Head, Eliot and Sylvia, you had a load of work."

She looked away. "Would you like some coffee?" She stood up and disappeared in the kitchen.

THE HEPBURNS

The next day I had an appointment, scheduled earlier, to meet the Hepburns. And so we all took the train to London. I would see the Hepburns, while my husband and son will be touring the city.

Stuck among the pages of Eliot's 1977 diary I had found the picture of a smiling seven-year-old blonde girl, bearing the caption "Dec. 20, 1977, sent by George, her father. Jessica, Anna's grandchild and my godchild". While I was corresponding with Hannah Kay, the Bishop's Stortford Museum curator, I searched the Internet too, looking for the little girl, Jessica Hepburn, and found an address. I wrote to this address and got a warm and welcoming answer.

We exchanged messages and stories about Eliot, and as soon as I had a date for my trip to England, we set an appointment. And so, I was to meet the whole family on Saturday, 10 July, at 3:00 p.m., at George Hepburn's house, 68 Parliament Hill.

In one of her messages, Jessica mentioned a person I might like to contact, a scholar called Joan Maizels who wrote a thesis on Eliot. She also gave me her telephone number. I called from Italy, and again from Bishop's Stortford, but could never get Ms Maizels on the phone.

It turned out to be a pleasant afternoon, the first of other occasions in which I would meet Jessica. I was greeted by Jessica's parents, and then we all moved to an adjacent part of the house, to meet Mrs Margaret Hepburn,

Jessica's aunt – an imposing and beautiful woman. Strangely enough, I had thought she would be older.

What interested me was to understand the period, the atmosphere in which Eliot had lived. Anna Wickham's family would let me into part of England's literary history.

Patricia was right. George Hepburn, though an old man by now, was still handsome. He still remembered the first time he had seen Eliot. He must have been six to eight years old. It struck him how masculine she looked, or, rather, wanted to look.[9]

> I don't recall seeing Eliot at Hove. It was later. . . . The first time I met Eliot I was a small boy. I was in the nursery. I remember looking out the window and she was walking down below, and she was wearing some sort of male clothes, black. She had a straight skirt and a sort of male jacket, a rather male hat, a round male hat. She was rather masculine in appearance, wearing a masculine outfit.[10]

There was something about Eliot that had always puzzled Margaret Hepburn, and I could provide an explanation: Eliot would wear long white straps around her wrists, and was peculiar about them. She wouldn't go out of the house without having wrapped them properly. Patricia had told me that the same arthritis swellings that would appear on Eliot's legs would also deform her wrists, so the white silken straps were her way of hiding the swellings. Even in old age she would want to look attractive.

We phoned Joan Maizels to ask whether she would meet me and talk about her thesis on Eliot. The Hepburns had met her, and actually had a copy of that thesis. It turned out Joan Maizels would not be able to see me. She was sick with Alzheimer's disease and did not remember having ever met Eliot, let alone having written about her. I suddenly felt that Eliot's isolation was total. Even the one person who had studied her works and written about her was now out of reach. I couldn't have felt worse.

But Margaret Hepburn was extremely helpful. Not only did she lend me her

---

9 Since I didn't operate my small tape-recorder on that day, afraid to expose my technical clumsiness, the following are notes I made during and after our meeting.

10 George Hepburn, conversation with author, July 2004.

copy of Ms Maizels's work[11] – so that I could try to find some detail that was still missing or a clue as to where Eliot's lost manuscripts might be – but she also helped me find my way out of an assumed blind alley. For the past couple of years, I had tried to locate Ms Alexandra Pringle, Eliot's friend and literary agent, but evidently wrote to the wrong addresses. Margaret Hepburn gave me Alexandra's latest address, adding that she remembered her as a beautiful and intelligent young woman. She had met her in the past, and remembered seeing her also around the date of Eliot's death. Alexandra was the copyright holder I had been seeking for so long.

We also talked about Sylvia, who had belonged to Anna's circle of friends. They, too, remembered that she had been involved in some scandal, and that it was in the papers. I wondered how she looked, and to my surprise Margaret Hepburn took out a book, *Soho in the Fifties* by Daniel Farson, and showed me an entry on Sylvia Gough, accompanied by a picture taken at the Fitzroy.

It was the picture of a striking woman, not young anymore, but one whose gaunt, elegant features were still showing her past beauty. Farson writes:

> Sylvia Gough had danced in the Ziegfeld Follies in New York. Surviving on a tiny allowance, Sylvia had become a near-destitute Fitzrovian drunk, passively sitting there alone in the early evening, but she possessed a gallant perseverance going to the public baths every day to keep clean. She was so emaciated that her skin was translucent, revealing her skeletal bones, yet she remained charming, courteous and grateful for company. I never heard a bad word said against her.[12]

I saw Patricia again the following week. I still had many questions to ask her and was not sure whether or when I could come back to England.

---

11   In her unpublished dissertation on Eliot Bliss, Joan Maizels quotes Anna's words, as reported by her son Jim; to Anna, she and Eliot were a "combination", as if there were "a psychic link" between them. Joan Maizels, "Eliot Bliss: An Appraisal of Her Novels" (MA thesis, University of Warwick, 1994), 40.

Joan Maizels died in 2015, aged ninety-seven. In the obituary, published in the *Guardian* (28 May 2015), her daughter, Judith Maizels, mentions how her mother, a well-known scholar, a lifelong socialist and feminist, as well as an accomplished pianist, "obtained an Open University arts degree when aged 71, and an MA in women's studies at the age of 77". Judith Maizels also added that the MA was based on her mother's research about Eliot Bliss. https://www.theguardian.com/lifeandstyle/2015/may/28/joan-maizels.

12   Daniel Farson, *Soho in the Fifties* (London: Michael Joseph, 1987), 80.

CHAPTER 6

The Last Years

Bishop's Stortford
14 July 2004

We had our comfortable routine, sipping coffee and talking about our lives. Then we began talking about Eliot's last years, and, of course, about the fate of all her vanished works.

"When I had to go into hospital to have my gallbladder removed, I always remember, I was lying in bed, and we had a homecare, Babs, and I had been sick, and she called the doctor, and he came and had a look at me, and . . . Babs, I can't remember her surname now, Babs told him about Eliot ("How about the other lady?"). He went in and saw her. He wasn't our usual doctor. He wasn't known to us, you see. And he went in and saw Eliot, and said immediately that she would have to go to the hospital too.

"Then, after my operation, they said – because she had become heavy and the lifting was difficult – and they said that 'You can't do the lifting'. So I had to find a nursing home that had twenty-four hours nursing care. And the social services would pay so much for care in the nursing home, but it would not cover the whole cost. So, what I did was I contacted the Royal Literary Fund, in London, and I phoned them and I explained the situation, because we needed another twenty pounds a week to be found. A very nice lady answered. She said that the Board would be meeting soon, and she would put the cause to them. And the Royal Literary Fund paid the twenty pounds. It is very well known, I think, that they help a lot of authors. They agreed to make up the difference. So that was a great burden lifted off my shoulders. I don't know what else I could do. I only had my pension – and twenty pounds was quite a lot, you know."

Patricia smoked quietly, while the wind kept rattling the window; it seemed strange, as if the wind awoke each time I came to visit.

"And you see, she had diabetes, and she became also blind. At the hospital, we went through a great deal of trouble to get the machine for the blind. But she would just say, 'Oh, no, thank you'. She couldn't bear it. And she didn't like to be read to. Oh, no. It was dreadful. She became blind, and that was, really, the end.

"You have been into her room, as I still call it. I used to put a chair at the bottom of her bed, and blankets, and I used to move her. There was another chair for her support, but several times, at night, I had to let her down, on to the floor. She had become heavy – we used to laugh. And I used to call the ambulance in the middle of the night, and they would come and pick her up and put her to bed. Yes . . . I knew the ambulance men very well. Oh dear, oh dear. Then eventually we had to put those contraptions on the side. On one side of the bed she had her table, with her little wireless – she always had a little wireless. And on this other side I used to have this extraordinary contraption. A frame. She had had several light strokes [by then], so she was not in condition. . . . I had to sort of block her in.

"We had a very good physiotherapist, Mrs Owen, Pippa. I still keep in touch with her. One Sunday, Eliot had a little stroke, and I didn't know what I was going to do – this was before we set up the contraptions. I didn't know how I was going to keep her in bed, at all! So I called Pippa, I said, 'What do I do, Pippa?' And she came with her children – her husband was abroad. Fortunately, I had some nylon rope, and what we did was we sort of roped her in. Dear Pippa. . . . Pippa was important. When Eliot had her hip operation, in 1969, they found out one leg was shorter. She could not stand up. So we bought special shoes. Then Pippa would come and give her physiotherapy in bed. We depended on her. She went to live in Lincolnshire with her three children. She still does physiotherapy, but she only does children with disabilities. Eliot liked her.

"We relied on these people, and also on the home care, because when they would come, I could go for two hours to the stores or the library. They were people she liked. You know, she frightened people. She had the same sort of quality that Anna had, even in old age. A very strong, imposing personality. Still, all sorts of people loved her. Often they were the wrong sort of people. She wasn't an easy patient, but she still had an interest in life. We don't realize how difficult her life was, physically, and yet, she was full of life.

"She always had all her things, you see – her wireless, her writings, her diaries – all around her. Yes."

Voices burst into the room through the open window – kids coming out of school.

"How many years did Eliot spend in the nursing home?"

"She died in 1990. I think she was in the nursing home eighteen months. It was an awful journey to get there. You get a train from Bishop's Stortford to Cambridge, and then you go round onto another little platform and get a train to Roiston, and fortunately the nursing home was six minutes' walk from the station, which was good. My friend Anna helped me. I was allowed to stay with Eliot at night, and the doctor used to come in and just stand and look at the patients."

"How did she take it?"

"Well, she did realize where she was, and I'm sure she hated it. But when somebody is in that terrible condition. . . . It was terrible. She was blind. She wasn't even able to eat. When I was there, I was able to help. But when I wasn't there, I don't know how much she would eat, or whether she would eat at all.

"She died in the early hours of the morning, and they phoned me. I knew the nurses. I had visited her two days previously, and I knew the end was coming. She wasn't conscious. She had been getting weaker and weaker."

She paused for a moment. "Occasionally Lorna, who lives in London, comes down and takes me to London. We usually go to the British Museum and whiz around to see our favourites before going to the opera. Coming back from the opera, we usually sit and have a drink. It is very pleasant. . . . She used to take me to see Eliot, 'cause she knew Eliot.

"When my sight will be gone, I don't know what it will be like. . . . Voices were very important for her. She knew people's voices, she loved music, she enjoyed keeping herself informed, in touch, the theatre, the books, the news. The time she spent in the nursing home must have been awful for her."

Those were painful memories, and I felt Patricia was also thinking about her own failing sight. It was time to change the subject, and bring back the diaries, perhaps the manuscripts or Eliot's family.

"Patricia, I want to ask you about her diaries: they stop in 1980. The last entry is July or August 1980."

"What was going on then? 'Cause I might remember."

I picked up my notebooks and flipped through the pages.

"Let me look. It was very interesting, because suddenly there were no entries. . . . Here. After 17 July there are only a lot of loose notes, mentioning Dr Lewing, then Dr Greenfield, Lorna Wiley. . . . Dreams she had about her past, people she met in the past."

⸻

We spent the afternoon looking at pictures. She had given me dozens of beautiful photos. Some were torn, some out of focus, some looked like they had been in water, but overall to me they looked wonderful, bringing back to life memories of a happy past.

"This is her grandma. She was important to Eliot, Grandma was. She loved Grandma. That was on the Lees side. She kept in touch with Aunt Laura, who was Lees. Uncle Arthur went on to live in the West Indies. There were several other uncles, and they died. Aunt Laura, she always kept in touch with her. And with Auntie Kathy. She was the youngest. She was a Thompson, not a Lees. She was Grandma's youngest child. She and Grandma used to go abroad together. Eliot kept in touch with her and with Aunt Laura, but the uncles had died. Grandma's first marriage was to Arthur Lees, and they had five girls, always hoping to have a boy for the title, a baronetcy – so it was always a joke in the family. She divorced Lees and married Thompson.

"Eliot said her mother had got on extremely well with him, because he was all for hunting, shooting, fishing. A sporty man. Later in life he had several strokes, and Grandma had a man taking care of him; they had separate rooms, she couldn't be with sick people. We went to see Aunt Laura. Aunt Laura did all the housekeeping, and lived in her own room and only had lunch together with the family on Sundays. They all lived together, at home, which seems odd. A peculiar household, with Grandma. She had her own little chapel in the house. There was an Uncle Arthur who came into the title; he had children, he is a 'Sir', Sir Lees. Eliot used to see *Debrett's* [guide to the Peerage]. Her mother was the daughter of the baronet. The original title was in Ireland.

"Family was always important. . . . Did you get in touch with Eliot's cousins, Rosalind and Prudence Bliss?"

"Yes, I wrote to them. Unfortunately, I have some difficulty getting university funds and travel expenses, so I'm trying to get some information by correspondence. Rosalind sent me a family tree and told me there is a Bliss Family Foundation and that I'm welcome there if and when I can make it."

"I seem to remember that Rosalind told me she still gets an income from a chemist shop in India. Eliot's father's father had these chemist shops. There's such a sad story about Eliot's father's sister, Violet, who lived in America and committed suicide. Eliot was very fond of her. It seems she committed suicide by drinking a bottle of Lysol. It was very sad, really. I've been told there's still a cousin in America.[1]

"Prudence came to see Eliot in the nursing home. Her father was a painter, David Percy Bliss, and her mother was also a painter, and I thought her mother was the better one. Yes, she was a very good painter. They used to live in Blackheath, in London, and we went to have supper with them at one time. And then he became head of an arts place in Scotland. My only sister alive, Maeve, lives also in Scotland, just outside Edinburgh. Yes, you must go and talk to them."

"No research funds, remember?"

She smiled.

"You are the person who knew Eliot better than anyone else in the world . . .," I said. "And you are giving me a living portrait of Eliot. I rely on your formidable memory."

"Oh, we were together for so many years. Her whole lifetime, dear. But her family, and of course the Hepburns, are important because *that* was a very important period in her life."

"Still, you'd been with her for sixty years."

"Yes, but . . . I do wish that she had been able to go back to London, because *this* life was not the life for her."

"It was difficult for you too."

---

1 Eliot's surviving cousin, James Gordon Greenfield, Violet's grandchild, lives in California, and is a good poet himself.

"Yes, but then she . . . Her being was important, you know. And her work was important. She should have had contacts that . . ."

There was a long pause, which I didn't feel like breaking. It was not cold, but the tree outside was bending in the wind, and we could hear the branches scraping against the window, whose glass panes crackled like little faraway bells.

ALEXANDRA PRINGLE

Venice – London
End of 2004–Beginning of 2005

In November 2004, towards the end of the fall semester, I approached Ms Alexandra Pringle by regular mail at the address Margaret Hepburn had given me.

> Dear Ms Alexandra Pringle,
>
> I am writing at the suggestion of Ms Margaret Hepburn, whom I visited during the summer.
>
> I teach English and Postcolonial Literature at the University of Trieste (Italy) and am currently working on Creole writer Eliot (Eileen) Bliss.
>
> Though other Creole contemporaries of Ms Eliot Bliss, such as Jean Rhys and Phyllis Shand Allfrey, are quite well known by critics and the public at large, very little is known of Ms Eliot Bliss. Even her only two published books (*Saraband* and *Luminous Isle*) are now out of print.
>
> I think her work should get the same level of attention enjoyed by fellow writers Rhys and Allfrey.
>
> There are no biographical details of her life that I could find and my great hope is that you could help me understand Eliot better.
>
> I am planning a short visit to London in January (15 through 18) and was wondering whether you might have some time to see me.
>
> Looking forward to hearing from you.
>
> Sincerely,
>
> Michela A. Calderaro

Her answer came by email, on 5 January 2005. I would see her at her office, 38 Soho Square, London, at 4:30, 17 January.

Bloomsbury Group is a publishing house whose books are extremely successful; its authors are mostly famous names, with some new voices immediately widely read. Alexandra Pringle is the one behind this success. I had not realized this while doing my research, but as soon as I had seen her current work address, I understood, and felt totally intimidated.

In those days the office occupied part of an old building facing the square. Since then the Group offices have moved to 50 Bedford Square.

It was raining, and I was cold and wet. Inside was nice and warm, with shelves upon shelves loaded with books. I felt at home.

I was not prepared to meet a young woman. As I had gathered from Patricia and from the introduction to *Luminous Isle*, Eliot and Alexandra had met in the early 1980s, prior to the books' reprints, and Alexandra was the editor of the series on neglected writers. I had wrongly assumed Alexandra to be now of a "certain age".

We talked for quite some time, almost the whole afternoon actually. Alexandra remembered Eliot as being somewhat frail, a description that was in stark contrast with what I had imagined reading her diaries and letters, and listening to Patricia's stories.

Eliot would never cease to surprise me. She was what she wanted to be – frail, strong, hard as a rock, manipulative, charming or menacing – according to whom she wanted to charm or impress, or keep at a distance.

There was not much Alexandra could tell me that I did not already know, but she offered her assistance, as Eliot's literary executrix, in case I would need help getting materials from libraries or private collections. And she granted me permission to publish any material I would find. She did not know anything about the lost manuscripts or *The Albatross*, but promised she would look into her old files to see whether there was something I might be interested in.

She had moved from place to place since Eliot's death, she said, and of course there were always parcels left behind, or left unopened for some time.

⟫⟫⟪⟪

Throughout 2005 I continued my search to find out where the Cobden-Sanderson archive might have ended up. I tried various university libraries, such as the Manchester University COPAC and the University of Reading

Library. Although they provided useful links, which I later used for other searches, they could not help my present search.

The person at the Manchester University COPAC suggested I try talking to staff at the British Library, since, if *The Albatross* had ever been published, there should have been a legal deposit copy. Also, they added, it was possible that, given the date, no online catalogue record had yet been created for the book. It would be worth asking the British Library directly if they knew anything about it. Most libraries still have stock that is not accessible through their online catalogue, and this often represents early twentieth-century material. I could also try the Archives Hub,[2] which grants access to materials in a range of academic libraries.

Another suggestion came from Mike Bott, keeper of archives and manuscripts at the University of Reading. He had not come across an archive of Cobden-Sanderson, and it appeared from a recent history of the Doves Press, which was run by Cobden-Sanderson, that the papers which survived were scattered in many different repositories. Marianne Tidcombe lists in the Preface to her book, *The Doves Press,*[3] a number of libraries where such repositories may be kept, including the Bancroft Library, University of California at Berkeley; the John Johnson Collection, Bodleian Library, Oxford; the Emery Walker Library, Cheltenham Museum and Art Gallery; the Harry Ransom Center, University of Texas at Austin; the Newberry Library, Chicago; Washington University Library, St Louis, Missouri. These are only the major libraries mentioned in her preface. Others are mentioned in footnotes.

Mr Bott then suggested I contact Marianne Tidcombe at the British Library Department, to ask if she had come across any of the letters I was seeking.

Unfortunately, at the time, my letter to Marianne Tidcombe was never answered.

2　See http://www.archiveshub.ac.uk and http://www.archiveshub.ac.uk/links2.shtml.

3　Marianne Tidcombe, *The Doves Press* (New Castle, Del.: Oak Knoll, 2003).

CHAPTER 7

❧

Sylvia Revisited

Venice

23 May 2016

With what turned out to be the last small grant I would get for my research, I planned another short trip to see Patricia in June 2006, just before our longer trip to New York, where, besides visiting friends and relatives, I would be doing research at Bobst Library. In the meantime, since the University of Trieste "Consorzio per lo Sviluppo Internazionale" had granted me a small sum for the restoration of the material Patricia had given me, I got in touch with an expert in cleaning paper material, Ester Manganotti. She had been part of a team that had restored burned and wet books of the Verona University Library; a fire had broken out in the library, and in an attempt to save the books, the firefighters had flooded them with water. She was young, likeable, professional and passionate about her work.

The estimate she gave me for her work was deemed reasonable by the Consorzio, so I left all the letters, manuscripts and pictures in her care, and would collect my treasure upon my return.

Besides what Patricia and the Hepburns had told me about Sylvia, I could not find any evidence, either of her marriage to an English nobleman or of her involvement in a murder trial. Before going to New York, I wrote to George Thompson at New York University, the most valuable librarian I knew, hoping he would remember me.

His answer came by email within a few days, on 23 May 2006. He had already done some research for me going through archives I could not reach.

Dear Michela,

I do indeed remember you, and will be glad to see you again.

It seems that the Gough who is in the Oxford DNB and who died in 1963 isn't the father-in-law of Sylvia Gough. The entry on him in *Who Was Who* says that his family consisted of 4 daughters.

This morning I had just checked the full-text files of the *NY Times* and the *Washington Post*. Just now I added the *Los Angeles Times*, *Chicago Tribune* and *Atlanta Constitution*, and found paragraphs that Douglas Burton, 30, a reviewer, was on trial for killing Douglas Bose, 21, with a hammer, because he had given Sylvia Gough a black eye; Burton was pleading insanity. The *LA Times* had a story on April 29, 1936, beginning "Sylvia Gough, once a beauty of international fame, returned to brief prominence today as the chief witness . . . ." The *LA Times* had another story dated April 30, 1936. When I checked for Burton's name, I found another story in the *Chicago Tribune*, also from April 30, 1936, saying that Bose had thrown a brazil nut that hit Gough. The *NY Times* had a story on May 1, spelling her name "Gouch" and calling her "a 42 year old author who had been living with Bose"; she told Burton about the brazil nut, telling him "she could 'bear no more'". This story says that Burton was found to be insane, and there was a note on the verdict in the *LA Times* of May 1, too.

All these stories were at most three or four paragraphs, and the paragraphs one or two sentences. None of them gave a date for the murder. If you need fuller stories, it seems you will have to find London papers. Bobst only has the *Times*; I don't know what other papers were being published then. There was a paper called I think *News of the World* that specialized in murder and sex.

Meanwhile, looking more carefully at a story that I'd glanced at earlier, I see that her father-in-law's name is given. The *NY Times* of March 27, 1921 had a story "British Beauty in Chorus." This said "Mrs. Sylvia Gough, who was formerly Miss Sylvia Comstead,[1] has just passed her twenty-second birthday, and is the wife of Captain Wilfred Gough, son of General Hugh Sutlej-Gough." The *Atlanta Constitution* on June 21, 1921 had a story headlined "Beauty in English Nobility Joins Chorus to Earn Living". This included a portrait of her, and said that she had been a model for Augustus John, and other artists. The show that she was in was a musical called "The Right Girl", and was pretty successful.

I will look up Bliss to get an idea of who she was.

---

1   Sylvia's maiden name is spelled either Cawston or Comstead.

Good luck with your work, and I hope I will be in the City during at least a part of the time that you will be here.

GAT

George A. Thompson

New York, Bobst Library

30 June 19–July 2006

Going to New York is like going home, and our trip proved fruitful, as it always does, from all points of view.

At Bobst I could read the articles George had mentioned. He was right. The reference to the murder trial consisted of only a few paragraphs. Interestingly, though, Sylvia was mentioned as belonging to British nobility. I could not find her name connected to the Sutlej–Gough family in any official document, and her maiden name was often spelled in different ways.

British Beauty in Chorus: Mrs. Sylvia Gough Leaves Society to Make Stage Debut Here

Mrs. Sylvia Gough, well known in Europe for her beauty and in society in this country, is going on the stage. She will make her début as a chorus girl in "The Right Girl" Tuesday night at the Times Square Theater. Her intention to adopt a stage career will be a surprise to many well-known families which she has visited in Newport and New York.

Mrs. Gough, who was formerly Miss Sylvia Comstead, has just passed her twenty-second birthday and is the wife of Captain Wilfred Gough, son of General Sir Hugh Sutlej-Gough. During the war she took part in several amateur benefit performances in London, and because of her beauty was much photographed. She said yesterday that she was going to take the small part because she wished to start at the bottom in a profession she admired, and that she had hoped to open without the general public knowing it until she "had made good." (*New York Times*, 27 March 1921)

Beauty, in English Nobility Joins Chorus to Earn Living

The Honorable Sylvia Gough, one of the most famous beauties of the Welsh guards, and daughter-in-law of General Sir Hugh Sutlej-Gough, who in turn is the son of an English nobility, has left her royal family and resigned her leadership of London society to become a chorus girl in "The Right Girl," the

Gaiety musical comedy which is now in view at the Times Square Theater. Aside from her social position and popularity, the Honorable Sylvia is internationally famous for her beauty, having been selected by [E.O.] Hoppé as the most beautiful woman in England, and having posed for some of the greatest artists of the world. Her portrait by Augustus John is now on exhibition at the Metropolitan Art Gallery in New York. She is the wife of Captain Wilfred Gough. (*Atlanta Constitution*, 21 June 1921)

A couple of pictures showed Sylvia as astonishingly beautiful. The journalists were right. No wonder people fell for her.

From Riches to Penury: Famous Beauty Who Dined with Kings

Sylvia Cawston, wealthy, beautiful daughter of George Cawston, millionaire partner of Cecil Rhodes, was the darling of pre-war society. She lived at the rate of £40,000 a year. Her fame spread over two continents.

She was presented at King George's first Court. She married a rich young officer in the Guards. A king and dukes dined at her table. She had the world at her feet. Today she is practically penniless. This is the story she told this week.

"The old days are a dream to me now. I've had a terrible time. I'll tell you how it happened. I was born with a golden spoon in my mouth. Soon after I was presented I married Wilfrid Gough, a young Guards officer. He was the son of the Governor of Jersey. King Leopold of the Belgians often dined with us at my father's house. I knew Lord Kitchener, Arthur Balfour, every one.

I used to travel abroad – Monte Carlo, Deauville, Nice . . . I had one house in Versailles and another in Paris. In Germany – the land I liked best – I used to play tennis with Prince Eitel Frits, the Kaiser's son. My portrait was painted by Sargent, by Orpen, by John [Augustus John].

My troubles began after the war. I was divorced. I went to New York. I got a job as a show girl in the Ziegfeld Follies. I married a second time. My husband is Wheeler Williams, the American sculptor. I lived happily, although the £40,000 a year of pre-war days had dwindled to £2,000. But I was happy . . . until three years ago. Then we lost all our money in the American slump. I sold my property to pay my debts. And here I am, dead beat."

Known as "Broadway's Loveliest" when her first husband divorced her, Baron Maurice de Rothschild and Mr. Bertrand Neidecker, an American banker, were named as co-respondents. No evidence was offered against Baron de Rothschild, and the case was undefended. When Sylvia Cawston was in New York she worked for a time as a mannequin. As "Marguerita" she was known as

"Broadway's loveliest." Her father, George Cawston, was one of the founders of the British South African Company. He died in 1924 – bankrupt. (*Queenslander* [Brisbane], 21 February 1935)

In the *Mirror* (Perth, Australia) dated Saturday, 19 January 1924, there is a whole page dedicated to Sylvia's first divorce. It is a long and interesting article, whose title and subtitles run across the entire page:

England's Most Beautiful Woman Ruined by Vanity
Career of Handsome Actress Sketched in Divorce Court
Her Head Turned by Constant Admiration
Mrs Gough Deserted Her Fond Husband
And Joined the Films
Her Gay Pursuit of Pleasure Ends in Court

The article mentions that detectives were engaged in spying on Sylvia's behaviour and lovers, and opens with a tabloid-like description:

Ruined by her vanity, the divorce court has freed the distinguished Captain Wilfred Hugh Julian Gough, of the Welsh Guard, from his world-famous beauty, Sylvia Phyllis Cawston Gough. A pretty face, an empty head, a weak character which could not withstand the flatteries of designing men have brought to a disgraceful end one of the most promising careers of fashionable British society.

He [Captain Gough] had decided to have her watched. . . . An allegation was made against a man of a well-known name, but I do not think it desirable to mention it.

But in regard to the other co-respondent, a man named Neidecker, an American banker, a conclusive case could be established.

Having collected all the articles and copies of microfilms, some illegible, found at Bobst about Sylvia and her stormy life, I now turned to other questions I felt needed answers: When exactly did Eliot travel to the United States? Was she staying with Cairn?

I realized, of course, that the exact dates were not so important, since what was important was that she had actually left Patricia twice, to follow her heart.

During what I began to call my "search for Eliot Bliss", while trying to solve this and other mysteries, I had written to Eliot's aunt Dolly Lees at the address Patricia had given me. My letter had been answered by a gracious gentleman, one of Eliot's distant cousins, John Porter, who was at the time reading through Dolly's diaries. In these diaries Eliot was mentioned a number of times; one diary note was written in September of 1936, when Eliot was in America.

Once again it was George Thompson who set me on the right track. "Try the National Archives," he suggested – and to the National Archives I went.

I recollect that day – 11 July 2006 – as being hot and humid; and the cool rooms on the twelfth floor of 201 Varick Street provided the necessary relief after my long walk in the sweltering heat. The entrance to the archives was on Houston Street, between Varick and Hudson, not far from where I used to live, but quite far from where we were staying at that time. I was so carried away by the thought of unveiling one of Eliot's many mysteries that it had not crossed my mind to use the subway.

The archives were to be moved in the fall of 2012 to the Alexander Hamilton US Custom House at 1 Bowling Green in New York City, sharing the building with the Smithsonian Institution's National Museum of the American Indian.

The personnel at the archives were helpful. After a thorough search of hundreds of cards in the card catalogue, which produced only one date (though I knew Eliot had visited the United States twice), somebody suggested I try the ancestry.com website, a database where one can query lists of all passengers who had ever arrived in New York City from foreign ports, from 1820 to 1957.

Though the database is subscription-based, access is offered for free at the National Archives facilities, and so it happened that I found myself in possession of two valuable records.

Listed as *Eileen Nora L. Bliss*, she arrived in New York aboard the *Europa* on 18 August 1936. The person hosting her was a Mr Nathan Ader Emerson, and "India" was erroneously listed as her place of birth. For her second trip, she was listed as *Eileen N.L. Bliss*; arrival date was 14 December 1937; place of birth was correctly listed as Jamaica; and the friend hosting her was Ruth Stickney – her beloved Cairn.

※※※

In the following years, I was able to collect more information about Sylvia, and with the help of the librarians of the Faculty of Education at the University of Trieste, Alessandra Carlin and Federica Moretto, I could at last reconstruct the full episode regarding this mysterious murder trial. (This is a good place to express my love towards librarians. Their work is one of the pillars of any research.)

We found more articles, with plenty of lurid details about the famous murder trial. Sylvia Gough had been a daring woman. She had led the life she wanted, making choices a woman in her position, and in that period, was not supposed to make. No wonder Eliot felt she was in the company of a soulmate.

CHAPTER 8

⟫⟪

The Poems[1]

Venice

2006

Since our first meeting, I would call Patricia at least once a month – as well as on her birthday, of course. As soon as I came back from New York, I called her to share with her my findings, including the dates of Eliot's trips to the United States and news articles covering Sylvia's involvement in the murder trial. I promised her I would visit her again the following summer.

In the meantime, I collected the material that Ester Manganotti had cleaned and filed: dozens upon dozens of letters, poems and pictures. I was overwhelmed by the amount of material I was supposed to go through. I needed a work plan.

The year before, I had mentioned to Alexandra Pringle my wish to publish Eliot's poems. She seemed pleased with my plan, and I felt confident that some publisher would be willing to bring Eliot out of oblivion.

The first thing was to decide whether to work on the poems or on the correspondence. I chose to go with the poems.[2]

There were two nearly ready collections, *Selection of Poems: 1922–1931* and

---

1 A description of the steps that led me to the discovery and retrieval of unpublished works by Eliot Bliss was published as "Finding Bliss at McFarlin", *Tulsa Studies in Women's Literature* 34, no. 2 (Fall 2015): 411–21.

2 In 2015, with Alexandra Pringle's approval, I finally published *Spring Evenings in Sterling Street: A Collection of Poems by Eliot Bliss* as a Kindle book, and in 2017, still with Amazon, as a paperback edition. What follows constitutes part of my introduction, 28–32, http://www.amazon.com/dp/B00T6UA3V6.

The Wild Heart: Poems 1922–1929, and then a considerable number of poems on loose sheets, which I filed as *Miscellaneous*. Due to the fact the paper they were typed on was flimsy and delicate, the poems needed to be copied. Two young scholars helped me with this task, Elisabetta Giotto and Maurizio Pezzanera, who typed and filed the manuscripts.

Over the years Eliot herself had considered many possible ways for grouping her poems, moving individual poems from one collection to another – suggesting perhaps that nothing is ever fixed, unmovable and unchangeable. So, forced to make a decision, I picked a few from each group, choosing those that best represented, in my opinion, the different aspects of her personality or stages in her life – in short, trying to second-guess Eliot's choices.

The poems reflect different states of mind and periods in Eliot Bliss's life: There are poems that bring to mind the Caribbean, where she was born and whose memory she would always carry with her ("The Scent of the Sun in Darkness", "Secret Swords"); others are dedicated to spiritual life ("The Chameleon") or to important literary figures, women who had an influence on her life ("The Power of Littleness", dedicated to Emily Dickinson; "To Renée Vivien", dedicated to the famous poet and followed by "The Sapphic Rhythm", which is a loose translation of a poem Renée Vivien wrote just before her suicide attempt and dedicated to her friend Baroness Hélène de Zuylen).

Bliss's language is rich and sophisticated. Her poetry is never sloppy or boring, her inventiveness with words is amazing and her metaphors are daring and extreme.

Some of the poems subvert religious evocations and transform them into sexual allusions, as in "The Transubstantiation" and "Introibo ad Altare Dei", with their titles' obvious, yet misleading, religious references.

The Transubstantiation

Wrap up my body in your wise thought,
That I may unlearn what I know and again be taught.
Transpose me into water and rain,
A scent on the wind or floating grain –
That I may unlearn this dangerous love –
Whose medium is pain.

Then when I am become a stream –
Seal me and fold me in some careful dream.
Lock me up under your floor
Where no mouse may explore –
But if you would have me be joyful and free,
Then leave some little aperture apart
Wherefrom I may drink the wine of your heart, –
Till drunken, it turns me again
Into water and rain.

According to the Roman Catholic and Eastern Orthodox doctrine, *transubstantiation* is the process by which during Mass, at consecration, Jesus Christ's body and blood are transformed into the Host. But in the poem, the transubstantiation of the title becomes the one of the body of the speaking "I" into water or rain, a "scent" or a "floating grain", wrapped up in the thought of a lover: "a stream, to be sealed and folded in a dream". Another strong, yet irreverent, reference to Christian symbolism in this poem is the image of wine, which here is not a symbol of Christ's blood but of her lover's, to be drunk by the poet.

This subversion, this ironic, if not rebellious, use of religious terms, reflects a view of the church as a cold and distant institution that seldom accepts into its folds the different, the challenging. This is evident also in "Introibo ad Altare Dei", whose title, besides its clear reference to one of the most pregnant moments during Mass – its opening, so filled with expectation and mystery – strongly recalls the opening of Joyce's *Ulysses* with its outrageously mocking tone. The opening line of Mass – In nomine Patris, et Filii, et Spiritus Sancti. Amen. Introibo ad altare Dei – comes from the Old Testament, Psalm 43:4, "Then will I go unto the altar of God". The speaking "I" of the poem, however, refuses to "pay allegiance to a frozen deity" and declares that when she will die "Abraham's bosom need not then embrace" her.

This set of poems was written during a tumultuous period in Bliss's life and clearly reflects the difficulties she was experiencing in her private life. But her harsh stance towards the church, as it emerges in these two poems, would grow milder over the following years.

Religion, either accepted or rejected, would always play an important role in her life, and though the church was a constant source of conflicting feelings within her, she would remember with fondness the nuns who contributed to her formation. Indeed, many of the dozens of poems found in her apartment focus on the years she spent in the Highgate convent, and are a testimony to both this fondness and her extensive knowledge of the Mass service and of the Catholic canon.

Selection of Poems: 1922–1931 is a complete typewritten collection that Patricia found in a drawer, and it is in almost perfect condition, accompanied by a table of contents. The poems were collated while Bliss was living with Patience Ross, at 1A Hill Side Road. The collection includes all the poems listed in the table of contents.

Natural elements – trees, leaves, rain, wind – and the overall presence of death give this *Selection* its distinct character. Many poems are directly dedicated to death ("Petition", "The Constant Lover"); others refer to it indirectly ("Night-piece for Maud"); in one, in particular, death is seen as the means of passage to another world ("Clear Country").

In the same corner of the house where *Selection* was found, there was another batch of poems, some of which turned out to belong to another semi-complete collection: *The Wild Heart: Poems 1922–1929.*

Finding part of what might have been a complete collection aroused our curiosity, and we hoped that retrieving all Eliot Bliss's lost manuscripts would provide answers to most questions about her life. I was looking forward to my next visit to see Patricia, and I kept her informed of my work on the poems.

The Wild Heart was kept in a big brown folder. There was a table of contents listing many poems. Regrettably, most of those poems could not be found.

In a few manuscript sheets, within that folder, were lists of poems grouped according to different themes: Trees; Nature, Place and Recollection; Death; Life; Love and Suffering; Fear and Battle.

The table of contents lists fifty-five titles divided into three numbered sections followed by a fourth section entitled "Prose – Thoughts" which includes six titles; and a final section with twenty-six titles, of which four titles are typescript, the others added by hand.

Two additional pages, both handwritten, seem to have been front pages. The first carries a handwritten inscription at the bottom: "Proposed selection over 7 years work in 'The Wild Heart' (9 sections)". The latter carries a dedication at centre page:

A.M.G.
(1868–1922)

Repeated at bottom right:

To A.M.G.
(1868–1922)

Clearly the collection is dedicated to a person whose initials were A.M.G., but whose full identity we could not establish. One possibility a woman called Maud, to whom several poems in both *Selection* and *The Wild Heart* are dedicated. Eliot used pseudonyms in her novels, so she likely used them in her poems as well.

Checking the various lists, we were able to determine that some of the loose poems we had labelled as *Miscellaneous* clearly belonged to *The Wild Heart*; we also considered as belonging to this collection a few poems that had similar subjects or similar use of words (as "Riches", which is clearly connected to "Riches Suddenly Encountered in Russell Square").

The manuscripts demonstrate the strength of this woman who, plagued by bad health and poverty, kept writing even when her fingers were deformed by severe arthritis, when faced with all sorts of difficulties, but who always hoped that someday, someone would read her work.

These poems touched me deeply; even without knowing *who* she was, any reader is bound to be profoundly moved by the emotional struggles expressed in her writings, by her acute awareness of what life promises us, but seldom delivers.

Two poems, extremely sensual and erotic, are dedicated to Anna Wickham, and written at the time of their meeting: "Use Me Thou with Beauty" and "Perfect Measure". These poems seem to shed some light on their relationship, or at least on Eliot's feelings for Anna at the time. Contrary to what everybody told me, including Patricia and Anna's family, perhaps Eliot did not see Anna as a motherly figure, but rather as an impossible lover – a goddess, as she would later call her – to be loved and worshipped in solitude.

Use me thou; with beauty
With the sea's edge on my mouth.
With gold-scalloped humour,
With the trees of North and South;
But never in languor –
And never in sloth –
For my whip shall perceive thee,
And shall not be loath.
("Use Me Thou; with Beauty", To Anna Wickham, Brighton and London,
Late Spring 1926)

The brilliant sun of emphasis
Gyrates across my way;
Winds have shrieked on this beach
Where now the dolphins play;
Palms move in slow delight,
Regard thou this, –
Sun of the trees,
Keep perfect measure with your kiss.
("Perfect Measure", To Anna Wickham, Brighton and London, Late Spring
1926)

Do these poems shed a new light on Eliot Bliss's life? Do we know now, after reading her poems, *who* Eliot Bliss was? The answer is probably, but only in part. The only known details about her life are those that she herself chose to disclose to Alexandra Pringle, in the introduction to the reprint of *Luminous Isle*. But those details, as in any autobiographical narrative, may or may not reflect the truth: they may or may not be a fictionalized truth.

The poems, on the other hand, though they may not reflect the *factual* truth, certainly reflect an *emotional* truth.

Patricia and I talked on the phone many times while the work on the collection was proceeding, and she was delighted at the idea that Eliot's work might be revived.

London and Bishop Stortford
5–8 June 2007

I spent two days in London, having set a couple of appointments with Alexandra Pringle and Jessica Hepburn. Meeting Jessica had become a pleasant custom during my visits, and we talked at length about Eliot and Anna.

Alexandra said she had retrieved something that belonged to Eliot and would give it to me the following day. Unfortunately, that day I was scheduled to leave London and go see Patricia. Since I was planning to be back before the end of the year, however, we decided to meet again on that occasion and examine the contents of the parcel she had found.

During my yearly visits, and our phone conversations, Patricia and I had discussed the other vanished works, wondering what might have happened to them. On the one hand, we both felt we accomplished a great deal: many letters, a novel and two whole collections of poetry had been rescued. On the other, it puzzled us that *Seti*, *Hostile Country* and all the other works were still missing, not to mention *The Albatross*, of course, and the Cobden-Sanderson Archive – all still untraceable.

"What happened to those manuscripts?"

The fact that we had looked everywhere – in each drawer, corner, shelf – and found nothing was really bothering us.

"Maybe she sent them to some publishers we are not aware of." I was trying to think what a half-paralysed old woman, who spent her last years confined to her bed, or armchair, could do with all that written material.

"If she had wanted to send a manuscript, Mrs Smith would have known, and she wouldn't have said a word to me. I still keep in touch with her. I know Nancy Smith. If she did things for Eliot, she wouldn't say anything."

"But then she would also keep a copy here, like she kept *Return to the Wilderness*, and the poems."

"I think we looked everywhere. But you can go and look again. Go ahead."

What I found had no relevance to our search for the vanished works, but brought images of what life must have been for Eliot in her London days: a pair of black gloves, those usually worn at parties, a small embroidered bag with beads, some white satin ribbons yellowed by time – all half-eaten by moths.

On my next visit with Patricia, after enjoying one of her delicious soups, a leek soup, she insisted I visit Mrs Smith and ask about any parcel she might have sent at Eliot's request. Her determination was contagious, and I began to think that, yes, Mrs Smith had the key to Eliot's mystery.

We called, and she was willing to see me. A taxi brought me near her house at 42 Nursery Road. She was waiting for me: a small woman, still full of energy. Her memory of Eliot was clear and vivid. She had liked Eliot a lot, and it was not a burden to take care of her – though, she admitted, Eliot was not an easy person to get along with.

Unfortunately, among the many errands she ran for Eliot, there was never any involving the sending of parcels to publishers or friends, and about which Patricia had to be kept in the dark.

I went back to Patricia feeling despondent, drained of energy. I still felt I had to find answers to a couple of questions, though.

"Patricia, one of Eliot's collections of poems, *The Wild Heart: Poems 1922–1929*, is dedicated to 'A.M.G. (1868–1922)', and I also found some poems dedicated to 'Maud'. Any idea who she might have been? I tried academic search engines, and also asked librarians to help me, but we couldn't come up with any name."

"Before I met her," Patricia recalled, "she lived for a period with a couple. The husband was John Gosse, a singer; the wife's name was Maude Gosse. But I also remember someone called Maude Gill. Her name just popped up in my mind. I'm sorry, I don't know."

Venice – London – Bishop's Stortford – Venice
May–August 2008

It had taken me more than two years to complete my work on Eliot Bliss's collection of poems. There was still some to do, and I hadn't even thought about an introduction. But I knew I had to start looking for a publisher.

Thanks to one of those fortunate turn of events – which I have rarely experienced in my life – a friend of mine, a fine poet and visual artist, put me in touch with an English publisher, who was not only interested in reprinting *Luminous Isle* but was also willing to read Eliot's poems and see if they too were publishable.

I couldn't plan another trip to England until August 2008, and I had only two days to see both Patricia Allan-Burns and Alexandra Pringle. I was curious to find out what material Alexandra might have found.

Patricia and I felt elated and proud regarding the possibility of publishing Eliot's poems. Over our "comfort soup", we discussed what title would be most fitting for the collection.

"Pat, what about 'Spring Evenings in Sterling Street'?" I said. "It is the title of a poem she wrote and kept revising between 1925 and 1926, before her meeting with Anna Wickham, when she was probably still living with Susan. Want me to read it to you? It's quite long."

"Yes."

"Spring Evenings" belongs to a group of poems that deal with the issue of homosexuality, often connected to loss, solitude and separation.

> On spring evenings
> In Sterling Street,
> Theo and Louisa did not always
> Have the blinds drawn;
> Very often they would only
> Pull the soft green curtain
> Across the window.
> Then, if we came quietly
> Up the dim secluded street
> About seven o'clock,
> We could stand on the pavement
> Outside the tall narrow house,
> And watch the shapes and shadows
> Moving on the curtain.
> Very still we would stand;
> Sometimes we would lean against the railings,
> Tiptoe, and breathless, waiting. . . .
> On fortunate nights
> We might see
> Theo's tall sinuous form
> Bending over the table not far from the window,
> Her arms outstretched over the newspaper
> Spread out before her.
> Her shapely black head bent,
> And those queer thin shoulders
> Hunched up a little.
> Sometimes she would stoop

To throw her cigarette end
Into the fire, or turn back
To make a remark to Louisa,
Who, sitting at the other end of the room
Would be reading her proofs.

Or we might see
Louisa rising from her chair
Cross the curtain in search of a book;
For a minute her shadow
Would eclipse Theo's at the table;
The bookcase was by the window,
Sometimes she would stand there
A long time,
Choosing the book she wanted.
Sometimes Theo would come to the bookcase
And help her to look for it.
Their two heads, dark and fair
Would be nearly touching,
Theo's slender arm
Would be thrown round Louisa's shoulders;
Perhaps they would laugh
At something they had just discovered,
And Louisa's head
Would rest for a moment
Against Theo's.
Sharply outlined on the curtain
We would see the two smooth heads,
Louisa's like a boy's, close cropped,
Theo's black and sleek, the hair drawn over the head
Covering the ears.
The shadows would part and divide,
Blending once more
As Louisa passed Theo
With the book under her arm.

But on other nights
No matter how long we waited,
We could not see the shadows

On the curtain.
The light in the room
Tantalizing and faintly yellow,
Would peep at us
Through a slit
Where the curtain divided
With a grim derisive wink.
We knew they were there,
Sitting in that still room,
Living the life they had made for themselves,
Calmly ironical of the things that had hurt them,
Removed from the gibes and mockery
That we had yet to endure.
And because we could not see them
That night or the next,
Anger would rise in us,
Fierce and insatiable anger,
Anger more bitter than tears.
We would say to each other,
"It's no use, things will always
Be like this;
Why do we come here
Night after night?
If we saw them we should be miserable,
The contrast between their lives
And ours would make us unhappy,
Theirs lived as it were
Inside a beautiful casket.
Perfumed with the security and sweetness
Of the mind at peace, in love
With its best object;
Ours, an existence
Sharpened by want and endless striving,
Exposed to the prejudice
And oppression of ignorance.
And if we don't see them
We go away dejected,
With a sense of isolation and despair,
Feeling outcast, and forgotten.

Then we would make our way
Down the quiet discreet street,
Our hearts tight, our throats
With an iron band around them,
Not daring to say a word,
Afraid of betraying emotion.
Perhaps it had been raining. . . .
Black and shining the streets
Like dark mirrors, and the moon
Would be rising over the city;
Into the blue spring sky
She would sail, oblivious, untroubled,
With her mocking sardonic smile.
On seeing her
We would take heart again,
It seemed to us that she knew
What we were, and what we suffered,
That she understood; tender, amused
Knew us, and mocked the earth for us.
We would walk home
Quietly sad, and dreaming. . . .

And so it went on
Night after night,
And all because
In Sterling Street,
On spring evenings,
Theo and Louisa
Did not always have the blinds drawn;
All because there was a chance
Of seeing one of them
Outlined against the green curtain,
Or perhaps both.
They never knew; and now
They have gone away. . . .
The people who took the house from them
Never even draw the curtain,
But we do not stand outside on the pavement
Gazing in at the window, anymore . . .

Later on, when I left, I was still emotionally shaken after having read the poem aloud, and perhaps not ready for Patricia's words of farewell. She kissed me and, while I was going through the door, said softly, "I wonder whom Eliot really loved."

The following day I went to see Alexandra Pringle in her office. She had found something, though she didn't think it was very important.

She laid the precious bundle on the table. I picked it up and stood there, another piece of Eliot's life in my hands but with no certainty about what I should do next.

Later that night, back in my hotel room, I called Patricia.

"Pat, *Hostile Country* has been found."

CHAPTER 9

Vanished Works Found

The package contained reviews of Eliot's books, some letters, a copy of *Hostile Country*, heavily damaged and moth-eaten, and the copy of a letter by Eliot to Peter Davies, regarding the book.[1]

25th September 1947

Dear Mr Davies,
Thank you for your note of the 16th. Yes, I did receive the acknowledgement of the typescript of HOSTILE COUNTRY on the 12th all right.

Its [*sic*] about this book I am now writing you. I dont want to bother you unduly when you are probably very busy with the autumn lists just now, but I would be very glad to hear as soon as you have read the book, whether or not you think it is your kind of book.

I am very anxious to get this book published [. . .].

I am well aware that this book is very different in style and contents to my two others. It was written with a certain deliberate straight-forwardness and I have used a good deal of vernacular and very un-literary language in it – partly because it mostly concerns a type of person who speaks and thinks like this – and also because I have written to be read. This may seem a strange kind of thing to say – but from my experience during the last seven years most people do not read books by so called intellectuals – simply because they dont understand them.

I want to be understood, not by any means because of the financial side

---

1   Most typos and inaccuracies occurring in the original letter have been left unchanged. Only a few corrections have been made to clarify the meaning.

of it, though of course one has got to live, but because one is living today in a very different world to the thirties when one could write for a special and select few – mostly other writers. This was very pleasant but it does'nt [*sic*] really get one anywhere.

Another thing is, that it is thirteen years since I've had a book published, and many of my own feelings about life have profoundly changed; naturally this is reflected in one's writing. I've been obliged to make a sharper and perhaps more painful contact with ordinary life and ordinary people – probably all to the good. These people are not at all stupid as the "highbrows" imagined them to be. I think it is Cyril Connolly who has written quite truthfully in "THE CONDEMNED PLAYGROUND", that American writers have a language in which they can make themselves understood to a large majority of people, whereas English writers nearly always write for only one class of people – the mandarin class – and use a certain kind of language, and that if writers in the future are going to be read they will have to use a language to appeal to a new kind of reader. I think and know from my own experience, that this is true, and I have tried to do it in this book. I may have failed, but I shall certainly have another shot at it.

I feel this explanation is perhaps necessary about this particular book I have sent you, so I hope you wont mind my writing it to you. There is a great deal about Class and Money in this book, but the people I am thinking of and have written about here are obsessed with both these things – naturally enough perhaps since they themselves are in the process of changing over from one class into another, and are not at all sure where they belong or even wish to belong. In London one may not notice this so much (Londoners are much more human anyway), but in provincial life its [*sic*] very noticeable, especially during and since the war. This is one of the things I have tried to portray. I feel also, that in this book, I may have said some rather harsh things about the English – usually from the point of view of strangers – such as the unusual Irish workman, Sean O'Marny. But all the same this is true. Whether I have put it over or not, I dont know. The same thing applies to the feelings of the country against the city – though this ought to be too well known to need stressing – especially during the last seven years.

I hope you dont mind my writing all this, but I feel and felt before when I sent you the book, though I was then too tired to write it, that perhaps it needs some explaining.

I still have four other books in MSS written in the 2 years preceding the Blitz of 1940 when I had to leave London, and indeed meant to type one of these – but I found that I had to write this book first, it was something that had to be said, as far as I was concerned. The other books belong to a softer light and a kinder day, and at present I am unable to touch them.

Your sincerely,

The letter can be read as Eliot's statement on the position of the writer, a sort of literary testament. It raises modern issues regarding the kind of audience a writer wants to reach and what writing is meant to be.

Sadly, Eliot Bliss's letter solved one of my initial questions regarding what had happened to *The Albatross*, which had already been prepared for publication and listed in the *Who Was Who* as published in 1935. In fact, *The Albatross* had never been published. Eliot had only had "two books" published.

One wonders what happened to it, and hopes that sooner or later the manuscript will surface in some archive or literary depository.

⪼⪻

Fay and Elsa, the two girls portrayed in *Return to the Wilderness* – the two cousins forced to leave London in time of war – return in *Hostile Country*, except that here Elsa, Eliot's alter ego, is called Elise. We meet Joel, a sculptor, who is based on Paul Beadle.

The epigraph chosen for the book is "What Inn Is This", a poem by Emily Dickinson:

> What Inn is this
> Where for the night
> Peculiar traveller comes?
> Who is the landlord?
> Where the maids?
> Behold, what curious rooms!
> No ruddy fires on the hearth,
> No brimming tankards flow,
> Necromancer, landlord,
> Who are these below?[2]

---

2   In the transcription of the poem, and of other original manuscripts, I am using Bliss's spelling.

Comfortably sitting on my bed, I began reading the manuscript. The novel, like her other two, is autobiographical, and describes Eliot and Patricia's arrival and experience in Spellbrook, here called Spellbound.

> *Hostile Country*
> Part One
> The Exodus
>
> The main street of Abbotts Abortford winds itself serpent-wise for two and a half miles through the narrow town, starting on the flat marshland and gradually and tortuously ascending uphill punctuated on either side by numerous alley-ways, once the pull-ins for the farm carts, carriages and dog-carts of the past, but now crammed on market-days with cars and farmers brakes.[3]

---

3 For an in-depth analysis of both *Return to the Wilderness* and *Hostile Country*, see my forthcoming article "From Wilderness to Hostility".

CHAPTER 10

Cairn's Letters

I then began reading Cairn's letters. There were so many of them. I wanted to understand what happened during Eliot's second visit to the United States, why she had to come back earlier with no plausible explanation, and why her relationship with Cairn changed after that.

Cairn loved Eliot with passion and devotion. Each letter is a testimony to the love she felt for Eliot and how she suffered because of Eliot.

Reading them was emotionally painful, each word was a cry for love that could not be reciprocated.

Bronxville
5 March 1937

My darling –
Here I am again in the Community Church at Bronxville – Friday afternoon – writing to you on a pamphlet called "Signs of Jesus"! Your letter by the "Washington" came this morning – picked it up on my way to the train and I want to take a few spare moments opportunity to write you, in spite of no paper or ink or anything except this note from Suze in the same post, enclosing a list of "Garvin" names for the studio advertising. If I go with her to this broadcast on Sunday night, it will be my first "theatre" or "film" approach in ages.

What I particularly want to say now, while your letter is fresh in my mind, is that you have misconstrued one sentence of mine which you say hurt you so: about wanting peace and quiet of mind and wanting you to want these things if – or when – you come. To think that by that I meant your influence to be a destructive one, is not only wrong but utterly ridiculous. But – when I want you here – or thinking of you returning – I remember how miserable you were before; how you couldn't work, not simply for poverty, but worry over Pat and your separation from her. And I feel, perhaps too bitterly, that this might be true for you again when you leave England – and merely want you if possible to be sure – because just being with me has sometimes I think given you some pleasure – but never contributed over-much to your fundamental happiness or peace of mind. And I simply could not bear to have you come here again and again be torn to pieces by conflicting desires. That is why, weeks back, I suggested you try to bring Pat with you this time. But I want you – if you think you could possibly be happy.

New York
16–17 June 1937

My dearest –
Your last letter hurt me deeply. In anger and full of recriminations as bitter as your own, I wrote pages in reply which I shall not send, your reproaches, your cruelty – yes, you have yours, too – your air of emotional superiority [. . .] made me feel that I could not support no more. I felt impelled to write all that I have forborne to write for eight months. Things I have refrained from writing, [. . .] things that I determined to forget – to ignore at least.

I have forgotten nothing.

[. . .]

You were at pains to have me understand you had no desire to part with Pat . . . . But you wanted both of us – it was difficult – we torn [*sic*] you apart between us – just as you and me torn each other. But the things that drew you to me were far less tangible, infinitely weaker, than those that bound you to Pat. You loved her differently – and in a way that was way much stronger than the things you felt for me. I[t] was slowly and in great pain that I gain that knowledge more than lip-service, this may all sound picayune to you, or a calling forth of the dead when too long a time after burial has elapsed. But here, for me, I come to that essential which is hurting us both at the moment, which makes you write letters like your last one to me, and has held me so hard and frozen for so long –

At long-length the day you decided to come to America with me. The day you told me you stood in my room, and I put out my hand I could touch you now – the tone and expression with which you informed me – "I shall not go unless I have my return fare" – yes, when this dream came true there was no danger I could understand it.

[. . .]

It was such a pain for you to part with Pat, I was seriously of the opinion that you would refuse to go to the boat. In those few days you were distraught in every way, over things emotional and material, and it was natural that for you I did not wish – that I understood.

But what attention you did give me was flavoured with an air of resentment – a kind of acid undertone new to me. Perhaps it was unconscious, perhaps caused by anything – or nothing – but it hurt. And I was faced by the realization of happiness, NOT completely, for I had hoped to live with you, to find (in my egotism) that you loved me alone – or at least sufficiently to want to live [. . .] [with] me alone. And there was of course no longer any question of such a thing. Still, it would be the first time we had ever been alone together for any considerable period. So here was my dream coming true (and it had caused me suffering which I hoped for its realization) and with every breath you thrust me farther away and clung more desperately to Pat.

[. . .]

And so with the tears and the pain you suffered on the boat and here, I saw at last, irrevocably how little I could count for happiness in your life. There are some memories I treasure of you here. Some few times when you seemed happy, or at least less torn by anxiety and the pain of separation from Pat.

[. . .]

When you left I stood there on the pier until the ship passed completely from sight around the battery, I was crying [. . .] my eyes were still filling with tears – but my heart felt like a huge black stone stung in the hollow of my breast – hurting me with a dry hard ache – I never seemed to get over it. The hurt of that realization that I contributed not in the least to your happiness.

The letters you wrote me were like those you had written me before. It would be the same again. Nothing had changed. Nothing but me – who had come to realize at last that I couldn't give you happiness not even any part of it – that for you could only be accomplished with both Pat and me – if I were to figure in it at all.

It was for this I urged you then, when you said you would again return, to bring Pat with you. This is the coldness that has happened to me, this is what you wouldn't see me through with patience – what I needed time to recover from.

[. . .]

It should be obvious to you that I still care for you: And have forgotten nothing. Not even the days when you shared and told me hourly that you loved someone else . . . .

[. . .]

Goodnight, darling. And God bless and keeps you safe always. I love you.

C.

However, when she went back to the United States, in December 1937, just a few months after these letters had been written, Eliot did not bring Patricia with her, as Cairn had almost begged her to do, and things did not work out at all. In fact, Eliot asked Patricia to wire some money for a return fare, so she could be back sooner than planned – without providing any explanation.

⋙⋘

I didn't know what to tell Pat, how to tell her – because I felt she *did* need to know what Eliot had never cared to tell her.

I picked up the phone and called her. The phone rang and rang; it seemed she would never answer. When she finally did, I felt at a loss for words.

"Pat, I've been reading some of Cairn's letters to Eliot."

"Yes, dear."

"I'll bring some of those letters with me the next time I visit, but I need to tell you something." I told her some of what Cairn had written, mainly about her dejected conclusion that Eliot loved and could be happy only with her, with Pat.

She kept silent. I could hear her breathing.

"Pat?"

"Thank you, dear."

"Patricia . . . I'll see you soon. Take care."

"Yes . . ."

⋙⋘

When I visited her, she simply took the letters in her hands, touched them lightly, then gave them back to me, without opening a single envelope.

"You keep them. Now, tell me about the publisher."

꙰

CHAPTER 11

Becoming Eliot

Throughout 2008 and part of 2009, I exchanged emails with "my" publisher and felt confident we would finally bring Eliot Bliss out of the shadows of obscurity.

1 October 2009

Dear Michela,

Thanks for the complete file of the poems and the introduction. I will look at both closely and forward them for a second opinion to our associate poetry editor. We are just about starting to make decisions about the Sept 2010 to March 2011 season, a process that needs completing by December, so you will hear from us fairly shortly.

With best wishes,

J.

Unfortunately, in the end, the collection was not accepted, being perhaps not in line with their kind of publications. One could understand why: Eliot Bliss is a difficult writer to "place" – she doesn't belong in just one single niche but can fit into many, perhaps too many, of them.

Patricia and I continued to speak on the telephone, and I visited her in Bishop's Stortford as often as I was able. It had been a long search, a "treasure hunt", as we often defined our quest, which had left us wanting to find more treasures, though we knew it was almost impossible.

꙰

In March 2011, in the *EACLALS Bulletin* (European Association for Commonwealth Literature and Language Studies), I found a call for papers for the conference "Love, Sex, Desire and the (Post)Colonial", to be held in London on 28–29 October 2011.

I sent an abstract of the paper I intended to write. I thought who better than Eliot Bliss to embody those words: *love*, *sex*, *desire* and *postcolonial*?

The abstract was accepted, though the final version of the paper would somehow be more elaborate than what I had first envisioned. I notified Patricia, and we planned to meet after the conference, so I could tell her all about it.

Through the summer I read, again and again, Eliot's novels and poems, trying to write something that would help the audience understand *who* she was. The problem was that I was not sure, after all the searches, the talks, the reading and writing, whether I actually understood her. And then, one day, I finally understood what I was really going to talk about.

My paper would focus on an aspect of Eliot's works that had not been explored. Not just her struggle to *conquer* her own identity, but also the *need* to express desire and the *necessity* of hiding it.

I decided to begin my talk with some photos of Eliot and of her family, ones that had never been seen publicly. I wanted to show the difference between the "girl in the colonies", and the "girl in London", a sort of before and after.

Among the pictures that Patricia had given me, I also had one I had taken of the painting of Rebekkah that hung on the living-room wall in the small Bishop's Stortford apartment. *Rebekkah* would serve as the central inspiration of my paper.[1]

⫸⫷

Desire and the expression of desire are always connected to Eliot's female figures, be it in *Saraband* or *Luminous Isle*. Œnone, Brenda, Joy and Rebekkah are described as radiating a strong sensuality, which is totally lacking in her male figures: "Her [Em's] own mood, exhilarated by Joy's presence at her side, the

---

1   What follows is a revised version of the paper presented at the London Conference, Love, Sex, Desire and the (Post)Colonial. See also my introduction to Eliot Bliss, *Spring Evenings in Sterling Street: Poems by Eliot Bliss* (Amazon Kindle, 2015; Amazon Paperback, 2017), 24–27.

swinging white-clad body, the pressure on her arm, rose suddenly to a higher temperature. Forgetting everything – Ellis, her engagement unannounced, the long hot evenings at the bungalow, the feverish nights at home, only the present, calm and buoyant, with Joy like a miracle flashed from Heaven – to be lived and enjoyed for an hour or perhaps less" (*Luminous*, 291–92). This sexuality that cannot find its expression in marriage. The realization of what she would become if married – "A husband. A wife. A bird in a cage" (273), "his wife behind the tea-pot, or at the other end of the dinner table" (356) – is what leads Em to rebel.

Rebekkah is perhaps the most interesting among Eliot's female characters. Rebekkah is the only one in *Luminous Isle* who keeps the name of the person who inspired the character, and she represents an important aspect of unfulfilled sexuality. The relationship with Rebekkah, both in fiction and in real life, never led to sexual consummation. Rebekkah, and all references to Eliot's attraction to a black woman and her community is highlighted in various parts of the novel, and the impossibility of a closer relationship is among the motives for choosing exile.

To Em, Rebekkah represents the perfect combination of sheer beauty and independence; the black girl's words, "Ah couldn't work for anyone but meself, Missus" (*Luminous*, 205), resonate deeply in Em's heart: "How well one understood that feeling." There is an evident emotional communion between the two girls. In Rebekkah's company, Em is "completely happy, feeling in solid harmony with the rounded and complete personality walking beside her" (205). The harshness of their departure is softened only by the promise of a second meeting: " 'Sunday – bringin you star-apples, Missus.' The tryst would be kept." (206).

And the second meeting will coincide with Em's realization of what her life might become if she chose marriage:

> "A bird imprisoned in a cage, forever and ever, body and soul, even one's thoughts belonging to someone else." (*Luminous*, 276)

> "Missus keep happy till Ah come agen." Rebekkah with a last smile going towards the kitchen, swinging her leisurely hips.
>   Keep happy till I come again. What was that? That was what a lover would say – a real lover, somebody who came not to destroy but to recreate. (279–81)

It is always Rebekkah – it would always be Rebekkah – to come between Em and the male figures around her.

> That was what she [Rebekkah] had been – daylight in the mind communicating itself to the heart. (354)

> Now, much later, she [Em] saw it all and understood. From the first it was Rebekkah who had been the stronger. [. . .] [W]hen she had let Rebekkah know, without saying so, that something was wrong. From the start Rebekkah had known, but in her plastic and inarticulate way she had never pressed the point. Too many things divided them. (354)

The blue mountains of Jamaica and its black inhabitants came to represent a shelter. Rebeccah, the black nanny in *Saraband*, reappears as Rebekkah in *Luminous Isle*, both portraits of a woman Eliot Bliss met on her journey back to Jamaica in 1923 and who became her friend. Her house in the mountains became a sanctuary whenever Eliot wanted to hide from the garrison people. Blacks offered Eliot/Em/Louie the warmth, the understanding, the closeness she could not find in her own mother.

The most violent scene in *Luminous Isle* shows Em being viciously spanked by her mother: "she felt a stinging blow on her back which quivered through the whole of her body. She clutched the bed and screamed in terror. It was not her mother – it was a monster out of some nightmare" (*Luminous*, 33). Whites are portrayed in the most unfavourable light. They are violent, superficial or downright racist.

At the time of the 1984 reprint of *Luminous Isle*, Bliss regretted not having listened to Vita Sackville-West and taken out some of the most racist remarks made by Em's mother – such widespread colonizers' views as "She's only a nigger. She'll be getting too big for her boots. I shall have to send her away", referred to Belle, Em's maid. (*Luminous*, 144). However, while it is certainly true that the whole structure of the book would have benefited from some blue-pencilling, from a historical perspective those remarks are important.[2]

---

2   The problem of decolonization and the clash between the black and the white communities, foreseen in Bliss's work, would be developed by Dominican writer and political activist Phyllis Shand Allfrey in *The Orchid House*, 1953. See Michela A. Calderaro, *"Beauty . . . sickness . . . horror:* L'isola di Phyllis Shand Allfrey" *Merope* 9 (21 May 1997): 99–115.

The book is Bliss's courageous attempt at distancing herself from those views. Creoles, like Bliss, were disparaged by both the white British-born colonizers *and* the black population. Furthermore, with her father an officer who was not a permanent resident but only stationed on the island, Bliss's family could not be considered part of the island's "aristocracy" – creoles who had been there for generations. Not belonging to any of the island's social communities (the black inhabitants, the wealthy colonizers and the impoverished planters) – and being relatively poor on top – she suffered a greater alienation than her fellow creole writers, Jean Rhys and Phyllis Shand Allfrey.

⟫⟪

In a search for the "literary foremothers" of today's women writers from the Caribbean, one encounters some difficulties. As Evelyn O'Callaghan states, "to consult most of the pre-twentieth century West Indian texts [she] had to travel to the copyright libraries of Britain".[3] Most works are out of print, not only those dating back to the nineteenth century, but those printed in the twentieth century as well.

Stressing the fact that West Indian women writers "did not emerge fully-formed in the 1970s", and that therefore there is a literary tradition to be traced down, O'Callaghan refers to Brenda Berrian's *Bibliography of Women Writers from the Caribbean*[4] and cites works by women writers, from the nineteenth century, beginning with Mary Prince's *History* (1831), to the twentieth century, when, "despite scant attention paid to the fact, women writers like Elma Napier and Jean Rhys from Dominica, and Eliot Bliss and Alice Durie of Jamaica, were publishing fiction in the 1930s. By the 1950s . . . the list had grown to include, among others, Phyllis Shand Allfrey (Dominica), Ada Quayle, Vera Bell and Cicely Waite-Smith (writing on Jamaica) and Celeste Dolphin (Guyana)."[5]

Reading this rich list of writers, one cannot but notice that Rhys, Allfrey and Bliss are the only *white* West Indian writers – three creole women whose writings are the expression of a deep alienation and pain that have not always been

---

3   O'Callaghan, *Woman Version*, 18.

4   Brenda Berrian, *Bibliography of Women Writers from the Caribbean (1831–1986)* (Washington: Three Continents Press, 1989), x. As quoted in O'Callaghan, *Woman Version*, 17.

5   O'Callaghan, *Woman Version*, 18.

fully understood, and deserve more attention by critics and readers at large.

The word to be underlined here is "creole". These writers dealt with problems of racial and cultural interrelation, with the impossibility/possibility of connecting West Indians of African descent to West Indians of European descent, and they are the necessary link between the two. When comparing the books, and hence the vision of the three writers and the destiny of their works, one should not forget the different historical contexts against which each novel was set and written. *Wide Sargasso Sea* is set in the nineteenth century and was written in the 1960s; *The Orchid House* is set in the 1950s and written in the 1950s, during a period of great change and hope for total independence in the Caribbean islands; while *Luminous Isle* was written in the 1930s, when talks of decolonization were still in the distant future and when it was unpopular to voice such strong criticism of white rule in the colonies. This might explain why the book "did not do well", although it was received with good reviews and had been backed by Vita Sackville-West and Harold Nicolson.

But there is one aspect that stands out when analysing Eliot Bliss's novels *and* life. While her heroines, following the same route she had chosen for herself, affirm their independence and freedom from the patriarchal order and refuse to assume the canonical role of wife and mother, they never fully carry out *her* life project. They never complete the journey towards that self-affirmation which *Eliot* sought and accomplished: to live in full her sexuality, fully aware of her choice. What her heroines lack is the articulation, or better, the *freedom to articulate* their sexual desire.

While writers tend to fulfil their dreams through their works – letting their characters achieve what they cannot achieve in "real" life, that is, they "live" on the pages of their novels – in Eliot Bliss's case, the opposite is true.

So, to a certain extent there is a dichotomy between fictionalized reality and biographical reality, between dreams and actualization of those dreams, sexuality fulfilled in real life and unfulfilled in fiction. Their incomplete performance is in stark contrast to the one accomplished by their creator.

Why was it so impossible for the creatures of her imagination to follow in her footsteps, however uncertain these might have been? Such a literary choice was probably dictated by the times and by the fact that she was a creole.

For years creole women in literature had been depicted in the most negative light – the series of mad creole women locked in the attics of the English countryside is endless – and it is only during the first half of the 1900s that the only three white creole women writers of that period, namely Jean Rhys, Phyllis Shand Allfrey (*The Orchid House*, 1953) and Eliot Bliss, as Evelyn O'Callaghan points out, "give voice to the agony of the creole's double alienation from 'native' black and European white experience, and detail in a unique way the ambivalence of those just sufficiently colonized to call both England and the Caribbean 'home'."[6] O'Callaghan's book is fundamental for the understanding of these writers, since it is also the first academic work to group together Allfrey, Rhys and Bliss.

Phyllis Shand Allfrey was born in Roseau, Dominica, in 1908, and also died there in 1986. She knew Rhys, with whom she kept an epistolary contact, but never met Bliss. She was a passionate political activist who made huge personal sacrifices for the Caribbean cause, and served as the minister of health and social affairs in the first federal government of West Indies (being the only woman and the only white person in that government).

Bliss's creoleness is expressed, and experienced, as an impossibility of belonging. What has been underlined in the last few years by critics – the double alienation of white creole women, their impossibility of belonging to a single cultural, ethnic or social group – is exposed in Bliss's works of the early 1930s, when the issue of creoleness had not yet been discussed or even mentioned. In the case of Bliss, the alienation is a *triple* alienation, because she was also a lesbian, just as her characters were.

What she exposed in her novels – describing the ugliness of white people, creating closely autobiographical characters, expressing sexual desires and voicing feminist views, portraying women who are aware of being "other" and their impossibility of getting together with those who share their "otherness" – was in those years almost like an invitation for resistance from the reading public. Allowing her heroines to live in full their diversity would have meant definite ostracizing – while all she wanted, for them, and for herself, was to be "sexless, creedless, classless, free" (*Saraband*, 371).

The question, which I had asked myself at the beginning of my search for the true Eliot, and which I would have to ask myself again, was simple: "Was she a British writer, a creole writer, or, arguably better, a lesbian writer?"

---

6   Ibid., 28.

As of today, I do not have a clear answer, though the words that come to mind when describing her are *revolutionary* and *daring*.

◆◆◆

With the outline and the pictures presentation ready, I called Patricia. As usual I let the telephone ring many times, but this time there was no answer. It had happened before, I told myself. She probably travelled to London accompanied by her friend, Lorna.

After a while, though, I began to worry. I knew I would be in Bishop's Stortford after the conference, but I would have liked to talk to her before getting there. I called again before leaving Italy.

The line was ringing, as it had been ringing for the past month, and I was ready to give up. I had been calling every other day since her birthday, as I had promised I would do. None was ever answered. But now, suddenly, someone picked up the phone, and an unfamiliar voice said,

"Hello?"

It took me a moment to react.

"Oh . . . Hi, this is Michela Calderaro calling from Italy. I've been calling for the last month or so."

"Of course! This is Sue Wilson speaking, Patricia's niece. We found your name and address . . ."

London – Senate House, Institute of English, University of London
28–29 October 2011

Our panel, "Reading/Writing Caribbean Confluences", was held on 29 October, in the afternoon. It was chaired by James Conrad, and included, beside myself, Victor Figueroa ("Desiring Colonial Bodies in Mayra Santos-Febres's *Fe en disfraz*") and Sue Houchins ("Queering Race in Its Commitments to Hardness"). I had thought I would be nervous, as usual during conferences, but when my moment came, I felt relaxed and confident, and opened my talk with an homage to Patricia:

> This paper, "Becoming Eliot: Birth of a Writer", is about a fascinating author whose works have been out of print for nearly thirty years. She is what we call,

a "neglected writer". I've been researching her work and life for some time now, and this paper is a brief introduction to my findings.

But before telling you about Eliot Bliss, I would like to publicly thank her faithful companion for more than fifty years, Patricia Allan-Burns, a dear friend who helped me understand Eliot better, and who died on the second of October, a few weeks ago, at ninety-seven.

~~~~

CHAPTER 12

Spring Evenings in Sterling Street

Venice and Derbyshire

2015

It took me a very long time to go back to what I had considered, years earlier, as *my* book on Eliot Bliss and which had become *our* book on Eliot Bliss, after my encounter with Patricia.

Without my annual visits to Bishop's Stortford and monthly conversations with Pat, I felt I had lost my partner.

Resuming work on the collection was not going to be easy, but it needed to be completed. I slowly began to check, again and again, which poems would offer the best picture of Eliot. The choice was harder than I had thought, but in the end I was quite happy with the list of poems that I wanted published. In 2015, *Spring Evenings in Sterling Street: A Collection of Poems by Eliot Bliss* was finally ready for publication, and the Kindle edition reached virtual shelves.

My hope was for someone to read and appreciate Eliot's work, and indeed that's exactly what happened.

Jacqueline Bishop, poet, visual artist and interviewer for "Bookends", the *Jamaica Observer* Sunday literary supplement, whose editor is writer Sharon Leach, asked to interview me about Eliot Bliss and her collection of poems during Poetry Month, April 2015.

The supplement (19 April 2015) not only featured four full pages dedicated to Eliot Bliss, but also published the poem that gives the collection its title, "Spring Evenings in Sterling Street".

The interview, "'White Caribbean': An Interview with Biographer Michela Calderaro on the Life and Work of Jamaican Poet Eliot Bliss", was well received, and many scholars wrote to me, enquiring whether any other poems or manuscripts by Eliot Bliss would be ever published.

My only regret was that Patricia was no longer here to share with me the joy of this renewed interest in Eliot's work.

But there was something else that Patricia had urged me to do, a wish that I could fulfil: She wanted me to get in touch again with Eliot's only surviving relatives from both sides of her family, her cousins Prudence and Rosalind Bliss, and John Porter on the Lees side.

My letters to John Porter were not answered, but Rosalind Bliss promptly wrote back and invited me to come see her and her sister at Hillside Cottage, Windley, Derbyshire.

Prudence does not live in Derbyshire, but I was told she would visit during my stay. What a wonderful stay it was!

⋙⋘

Rosalind and I had corresponded over the years, and she had mentioned that her sister Prudence was active in the Bliss Family History Society.

The society runs a useful website, www.BlissFHS.co.uk, a treasure trove of information about the origins of the family, especially their Bliss Genealogical Data Base, and a great resource for scholars.

As reported on the website,

> P.H. Reaney, the authority on English surnames, derives [the Bliss] name from either the Middle English noun blisse, joy or gladness, or from the Norman family of de Blez."[1] No records report the name de Blez after the fifteenth century.
>
> English state and ecclesiastical documents record de Blezes in the counties of Hereford, Worcester and Warwicks in the twelfth century. It is thought the name originates from Blay, a village nine kilometres west of Bayeux in Calvados, Normandy. The de Blezes came to the Welsh March in the service of Adam

---

[1]   The Bliss Family History Society, "Origins of the Bliss Name", http://www.blissfhs.co.uk/origins.htm.

de Port, baron of Kington, circa 1115. Later, they were knights in the service of the barony of Radnor, owing allegiance first to the de Braose baronial family and later to the Mortimers of Wigmore, who inherited Radnor by marriage to the de Braose heiress. One of the manors held by William de Blez in the 1160s was Stok in Herefordshire, which became known as Stoke de Blez and then Stoke Bliss, clearly demonstrating the transition of Blez into Bliss. The Bliss manor in Staunton on Wye is also named from its de Bleez or de Blees medieval landlords. We are confident many modern Blisses and Bleases share a common rootstock in the Norman family of de Blez. The second source of our name probably originates in more easterly counties of England. In the reign of Henry II (1154–1189), a "Richard callyd Blisse" held land at Parndon in Essex from the Knights Hospitallers of St John of Jerusalem. It sounds as though Richard had only recently come by his last name. The usage of the Bliss name quickly became widespread. In 1225 a Bliss landholding at Cirencester Gloucs. was mentioned in a customal in the Curia Regis. By 1270 (The Hundred Roll of Edward I), Blisses are recorded at Tyringham in Buckinghamshire and Waterbeach in Cambridgeshire. These were undoubtedly native English stock, being villeins or freemen of a lower order than the de Blez family.[2]

▶▶◀◀

As Patricia told me, both Douglas Percy Bliss (1900–1984) and his wife Phyllis Dodd (1899–1995) were painters, both extremely talented. Their paintings welcomed me at Rosalind's cottage in Derbyshire. I was particularly stunned by Phyllis Dodd's self-portrait, and by her portrait of Douglas Bliss, simply titled *Bliss* and painted at the time of their first meeting. I was later to learn that they often contributed to each other's works.[3]

The cottage is surrounded by a garden and an orchard, and Rosalind's studio is the same studio her mother and father shared in the past.

---

2   Ibid.

3   An example can be seen in Douglas Percy Bliss's painting *Gunhills, Windley* (1946–52), now at the Tate Gallery. A paragraph in the catalogue entry reads: "It was painted from the motif, without any sketches, from his [Bliss's] bedroom window on the first floor of Hillside Cottage . . . [and] represents part of the Blisses' own garden (a lane, running between the two hedges, divides it from Yew Cottage). At the lower right corner appear the figures of the artist's daughters Prudence . . . and Rosalind . . ., wearing the gym tunics of their nearby school. They were painted in this picture by their mother Phyllis Dodd." *The Tate Gallery 1980–82: Illustrated Catalogue of Acquisitions* (London: Tate Galery, 1984).

While I had known about Douglas's and Phyllis's art, I had hardly expected to see such a great amount of talent passed on to their daughters. It was only during a search that I had done prior to my visit to Windley that I found the ripeness of Rosalind's paintings and the skill displayed by Prudence in her window decoration – which is far more than ordinary decoration: it is art. When I met them, I was surprised at their humble behaviour, devoid of any self-congratulatory celebration of their accomplishments.

We spent the weekend looking at pictures, talking about art, their family and heritage. On my last Sunday, they took me on a splendid tour of Haddon Hall. As had happened with Patricia, I felt as welcomed as a family member.

With cups of tea in our hands, a regal cat, Jeff, baking in the warm sun, the pile of pictures in front of us, we sat together trying to find out who was who in the family. Unfortunately, we had little success trying to match faces to names. But to my surprise, I discovered that besides what I had found on the Bliss Family History Society website, the more modern descendants of the Bliss family had many branches coming down from the patriarch John Bliss (b. 1783 or 1786) who had married Elizabeth Worcester (1723–97).

The story of the family is a fascinating one, which I have summarized in the Appendix as best I could based on Prudence's notes and terrific memory, a couple of family trees with explanatory notes written by Douglas Percy Bliss, and additional details provided by James Gordon Greenfield.

CHAPTER 13

※»⪼⪻«※

The Mermaid

My hope is that this work will shed some light on Eliot Bliss's life and raise interest in her works, so that other scholars may continue the search for her still-lost manuscripts, and those that have been rescued may be published and read. These are works which prove her incredible talent and courage in dealing with sensitive subjects, adversities and ostracism, and which can finally demonstrate her literary stature and courageous fight, often misunderstood and misinterpreted, against any kind of discrimination.

In the endless quest for identity, Bliss would choose to free herself from the burdens of sex, religion and class, and in order to do so, she had to let her soul "emerge out of the flesh" (*Saraband*, 301) or, better, "shed her body" (310) like a mermaid. Like mermaids in other creole women writers' works,[1] she would "cast off her flesh [and] lose scales", "The shadow of [her] scales / Will always remain" but "The sea will never take [her] back."[2]

The allusions to the mermaid, a creature that is neither woman nor fish, that belongs to neither sea nor land and in whose eyes one can see the "rich, clear, luminous depth of blue-green, like the colour of the sea" (*Luminous*, 6), is recurrent in Bliss's novels. She herself belonged neither to Britain nor to the West Indies, neither to the white nor to the black community. Her choice would ultimately offer an answer to her lifelong quest: she would now be living "sexless, creedless, classless, free" (*Saraband*, 371).

---

1   See my forthcoming book, *The Mermaid in Caribbean Literature*.

2   Shara McCallum, *The Water Between Us: Poems* (Pittsburgh: University of Pittsburgh Press, 1999), 84–85.

Bliss Family

Let us begin with the patriarch, John Bliss (b. 1723 Whittleby, Northamptonshire, England; d. 1783 or 1786, Potterspury, Northamptonshire). On 16 September 1747 he married Elizabeth Worcester (b. 1720 or 1723; d. 1797, Potterspury), they had six children, who were all born and died in Potterspury. The dates of their birth and death are not sure.

Sarah Bliss (b. c.12 January 1749)
Thomas Bliss (b. c.1755; d. 1819)
Mary Bliss (b. c.26 June 1756)
John Bliss (b. c.20 May 1764; d. July 1764)
Mary Bliss (b. c.20 May 1764)
William Bliss (b. c.May 1764)

Their second born, Thomas Bliss (b. c.1755; d. 1819), married Elizabeth Dickens, and one of their children, John Bliss (1794–1859), who ran a coaching inn at Northampton, married Sarah Cook (1796–1841).

According to the precious information provided by Prudence, Rosalind and Percy Douglas Bliss's notes, they had eight children. One of them, according to other notes by James Gordon Greenfield, was John Noah Bliss (b. 1833), who settled in Henry County (Ohio, United States) in the 1850s, and died there in 1900 or 1901.[1] Another was Thomas J. Bliss, also known as Old Tom Bliss

---

1   According to James Gordon Greenfield's notes, John Noah Bliss was buried in Hoy Cemetery in Shunk, Harrison County, Ohio, along with his first wife, Catherine (Cassie)

(b. 10 May 1821, Stony Stratford, Buckinghamshire; d. 1 January 1900; buried at Dyke), who was probably the third and eldest surviving son.

Old Tom married twice and had sixteen children, all born at Logiebuchany Cottage, Darnaway.

He worked as coachman for the Earl of Moray, and when sent North at Darnaway Castle, in Morayshire, Scotland, site of the Earl's home, he met and married (22 November 1844) his first wife, Jessie Sim (b. 1822; d. 17 September 1860, also buried at Dyke) who was a ladies' maid at the Earl of Moray's mansion. Old Tom worked as head coachman for the Moray family for sixty years.

There is a funny anecdote reported in Percy Douglas Bliss's notes, that at "his funeral the horses stopped outside the pub on their way to Dyke."

Old Tom Bliss and Jessie Sim were Eliot Bliss's great-grandparents. They had seven children (see also Family Tree of first family):

Thomas (b. Darnaway, 28 November 1845; d. 23 February 1907, buried London). Eliot Bliss's grandfather and James Gordon Greenfield's great-grandfather.
Sarah (b. 21 September 1847; d. and buried Australia)
John (b. 30 September 1849; d. 30 June 1906, buried Forres)
James (b. 13 November 1851; d. 1884, buried Dyke)
Jessie (b. 25 May 1854; d. 1927, buried Edinburgh)
William (b. 30 June 1857; d. 1918, buried London)
George (b. 7 January 1860; d. 1943, buried London)

On 14 June 1861, after his first wife died, Old Tom Bliss married Elizabeth Dawson (b. 1837 or 1838; d. 1923, buried Dyke) the maid of the manse. They had nine children (see also Family Tree of second family):

Frank (b. 30 April 1862; d.1946, buried England)
Elizabeth (b. 21 February 1864; d. 7 March 1896, buried Dyke)
Helen (b. 21 July 1865; d. 1922; buried Inverness)
Joseph (b. 25 November 1869; d. July 1934 or 1936; buried Mauchline). Prudence and Rosalind's grandfather.

Carter Bliss. John was later married to Charity Thorn and had a son named George, who married Alavander (no family name is provided).

Ann Stuart (b. 30 August 1867; d. 1939, buried Sheffield)
Daniel (b. 15 April 1871; d. 1938, buried Swansea)
Albert (b. 26 May 1874; d. 1964, buried Banchory)
Alfred (b. 22 March 1876; d. 1934, buried Dyke)
Henry (b. 9 July 1877; d.1895, buried Dyke)

Thomas (1845–1907), Eliot's grandfather, the first born of the first family, started to work at a chemist's shop at Nairn, and then moved to India. He opened different chemist shops, which he called *Plomers*, in Delhi and Simla, and also Lahore, which is now part of Pakistan, and made a fortune. His half-brothers, Frank and Joseph, had also moved to India and had joined him in the chemist business, becoming very successful.

Thomas married Sarah J. Teehan, in Bengal, 1868, the daughter of an army major. They had five children, Mary, Violet, Gordon, John Plomer and Randolph Stuart, all born in India. Being what we may call a free spirit and being prone to betray his wife, married life would certainly not suit him very well. And indeed, after some turmoil created by a lady, a Miss Gibbon, his children's governess, his wife moved back to London with their children, under the pretence to have them study in London.

Not much is known of Mary, not even her dates of birth and death, only that she married Horace Wyatt and in 1910 had a son, Digby, who married a woman named Minnie, and later died in 1977 in Dorset, England.

Violet Gladys (born in Lahore, 3 February 1884, died in California, 25 December 1930), grandmother of Eliot's cousin, James Gordon Greenfield (1951–), had a tragic life. Her husband, James Greenfield (1870–1940) whom she married in 1920, was a violent and abusive man, who would beat her up repeatedly. She took her own life with poison. In a letter sent to Eliot and Patricia, dated 30 January (probably 1931), a family friend, Ellen Bryant, states that she died of arsenical poisoning. She left one son, also named James Gordon Greenfield (25 September 1922–9 July 1956).

Thomas's three sons, Gordon Cumming (?–1949), John (Jack) Plomer (?–1952) and Randolph Stuart (?–1936), were sent to boarding school, to prepare for an army career. However, while Gordon and John Plomer succeeded in entering Sandhurst, Randolph Stuart, failed his entry exam, and went to work for a while in a bank in London, though without much success.

After this failure, his father summoned him back to Simla to work in the *Plomers* chemist shop. In the meantime, Thomas and Joseph had a fall out and Joseph had opened his own chemist business in Karachi.

Randolph (also known as Rafe), who had his own fall out with his father decided to move to Karachi to work for his uncle Joseph. He actually ended up running Joseph's shop in Quetta, the J. Bliss Quetta.

John Plomer became a colonel in the West India Regiment, married Eva Janet Lees, moved first to Jamaica, then to Sierra Leone and then to South Africa, where he died in 1952. They had two children, Eileen (Eliot), who was born in Jamaica in 1903 and John Jr Alexander Plomer, also known as Sonny, born in Jersey in 1909.

According to the notes by Prudence Bliss, though the family would not leave Jamaica until the late 1920s, the fact that John Jr was born in the Channel Islands might have been due to the fact that the regiment would offer "leave of absences" in certain cases, to help cope with the stress and difficulties of life in the colonies.

It is not unreasonable then that Eva Lees would decide to take advantage of this opportunity for the birth of her second child. John Jr, who became a police officer, had two daughters, Sally, who, according to various entries in Eliot's diaries, would often visit her in Bishop's Stortford, and Sue. John Jr died in Sierra Leone.

1. *Family patriarch Thomas Bliss, his second wife, Elizabeth (Dawson), and seven of their nine children at Logiebuchany, Forres, Morayshire, circa 1891*

2. *Eliot Bliss; her mother, Eva Lees; and grand-mother Mrs Lees*

3. *Eliot Bliss's father, John Plomer Bliss, mother and brother, John ("Sonny")*

4. *Mrs Lees, Eliot Bliss's grandmother*

5. *Aunt Laura Lees*

6. *Violet Bliss (Eliot Bliss's aunt), her husband,
James Greenfield, and son, James Gordon Greenfield (father of James Gordon Greenfield Jr)*

7. *Eliot Bliss aged two, September 1905*

8. *Eliot Bliss with her mother*

9. *Eliot Bliss as a child with her mother and brother, John, in Kingston, Jamaica*

10. *Eliot Bliss and her brother, John*

11. *Eliot Bliss as a young girl, Kingston, Jamaica*

12. *Eliot Bliss*

13. *Eliot Bliss as a young girl, Kingston, Jamaica*

14. *Eliot Bliss as a young girl, Kingston, Jamaica*

15. *Eliot Bliss as a young girl, Kingston, Jamaica*

16. *Eliot Bliss as a young girl, Kingston, Jamaica*

17. *Susan Curtnoys*

18. *Cairn, Massachusetts, September 1947*

19. *Cairn, Massachusetts, October 1950*

20. Cairn, Bishop's Stortford

21. Anna Wickham

22. Anna Wickham's son James Hepburn

23. *Anna Wickham's son George Hepburn*

24. *Eliot Bliss, London, 1930s*

25. *Patricia Allan-Burns at the time of her meeting with Eliot Bliss in the early 1930s*

26. *Eliot Bliss, London, 1930s*

27. Eliot Bliss, late 1980s

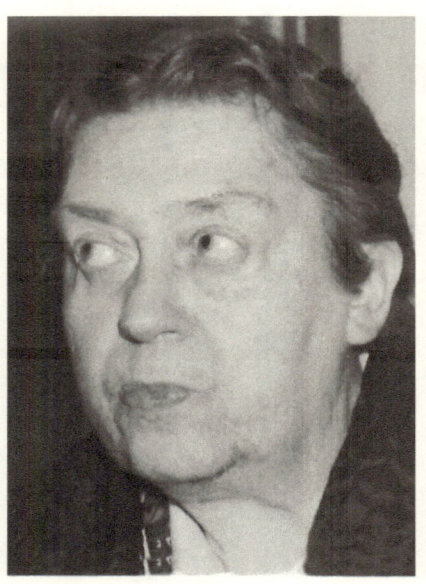

28. Eliot Bliss, late 1980s

29. Patricia Allan-Burns, Bishop's Stortford, 2006

30. Patricia Allan-Burns outside the house she shared with Eliot Bliss, Bishop's Stortford, 2006

31. Eliot Bliss, watercolour, Jamaica

32. *Eliot Bliss, watercolour, Jamaica*

33. *Eliot Bliss, watercolour, Jamaica*

34. *Eliot Bliss, watercolour, Jamaica*

35. Rebecca, *a painting by V.M. Jones*

Bibliography

Allfrey, Phyllis Shand. *The Orchid House*. 1953. Reprint, London: Virago, 1982.

Angier, Carole. *Jean Rhys*. London: André Deutsch, 1990.

Bailey, Paul. Introduction to *Saraband* by Eliot Bliss. 1931. Reprint, London: Virago, 1984.

Berrian, Brenda. *Bibliography of Women Writers from the Caribbean (1831–1986)*. Washington: Three-Continents Press, 1989.

Bliss, Eliot. "Hostile Country". Manuscript, n.d.

———. *Luminous Isle*. 1934. Reprint, London: Virago, 1984.

———. "Return from the Wilderness". Manuscript.

———. *Saraband*. 1931. Reprint, London: Virago, 1984.

Bromley, Robin. Review of *Saraband*, by Eliot Bliss. *New York Times Book Review*, 3 May 1987, 44.

Brown, Sally, and David R. Brown. *A Biography of Mrs Marty Mann: The First Lady of Alcoholics Anonymous*. Center City, Minn.: Hazelden, 2001.

Calderaro, Michela A. *"Beauty [. . .] sickness [. . .] horror*. L'isola di Phyllis Shand Allfrey". *Merope* 9, no. 21 (May 1997): 99–115.

———. "Finding Bliss at McFarlin". *Tulsa Studies in Women's Literature* 34, no. 2 (Fall 2015): 411–21.

———. "Islands, Colors and Obsessions: The Other and the Self in Three Creole Writers: Eliot Bliss, Phyllis Shand Allfrey and Jean Rhys". In *Rites of Passage: Rational/Irrational, Natural/Supernatural, Local/Global*, edited by C. Nocera, G. Persico and R. Portale, 97–103. Soveria Mannelli: Rubbettino, 2003.

———, ed. *Spring Evenings in Sterling Street: Poems by Eliot Bliss*. Amazon Kindle, 2015; Amazon Paperback, 2017.

———. "To Be Sexless, Creedless, Classless, Free. Eliot Bliss: A Creole Writer". *A Goodly Garlande: In onore di Sergio Perosa. Annali di Ca' Foscari* 42, no. 4 (2003): 109–20.

Dunn, Michael. *New Zealand Sculpture: A History*. Auckland: Auckland University Press, 2019.

Farson, Daniel. *Soho in the Fifties*. London: Michael Joseph, 1987.

Foreman, Lewis, ed. *The John Ireland Companion: Interviews with Friends and Contemporaries of Ireland*. 1986. Reprint, Woodbridge, Suffolk: Boydell, 2011.

Fromm, Gloria G., ed. *Windows on Modernism: Selected Letters of Dorothy Richardson*. Athens: University of Georgia Press, 1995.

Hepburn, James. Preface to *The Writings of Anna Wickham: Free Woman and Poet*, edited by R.D. Smith. London: Virago, 1984.

Maizels, Joan. "Eliot Bliss, 1903–1990: An Appraisal of Her Novels". MA thesis, University of Warwick, 1994.

McCallum, Shara. *The Water between Us: Poems*. Pittsburgh: University of Pittsburgh Press, 1999.

"Moods". Review of *Saraband* by Eliot Bliss. *Saturday Review of Literature* 8 (1931): 8.

O'Callaghan, Evelyn. *Woman Version: Theoretical Approaches to West Indian Fiction by Women*. New York: St Martin's Press, 1993.

Rhys, Jean. *Wide Sargasso Sea*. 1966. Reprint, London: Penguin, 1990.

Ross, Patience. *Black Bread*. Oxford: Basil Blackwell, 1929.

Ross, Patience. *The Glass Rose*. Oxford: Basil Blackwell, 1930.

Tidcombe, Marianne. *The Doves Press*. New Castle, Del.: Oak Knoll, 2003.

Tinsley, Omise'ke Natasha. *Thiefing Sugar: Eroticism between Women in Caribbean Literature*. Durham, NC: Duke University Press, 2010.

Vaughan Jones, Jennifer. *Anna Wickham: A Poet's Daring Life*. Lanham, NY: Madison, 2003.

Wickham, Anna. "A First Meeting with God". Memoir, c.1965.

Wyndham, Francis, and Diana Melly, eds. *The Letters of Jean Rhys*. London: André Deutsch, 1984.

Acknowledgements

My thoughts right now are with Patricia Allan-Burns, Eliot Bliss's companion, who had been instrumental in retrieving some of Bliss's manuscripts, photos and drawings, and who trusted me to take care of them. Over the years we became friends and shared the hope that Eliot Bliss could be rediscovered by critics and readers.

I have no words to explain how extremely grateful I am to the Eliot Bliss Estate, without which I could not have been able to publish Bliss's poems, and whose encouragement has always been important during my journey in search of Bliss's work.

I would like to thank Eliot Bliss's family, her cousins Rosalind and Prudence Bliss, and James Greenfield who granted me permission to publish photos of the Bliss family; Anna Wickham's grandchildren, specifically Harriet and Jessica Hepburn, who gave me permission to publish photos of the Wickham Hepburn's family.

The research on which this book is based could never have been accomplished without grants from the Italian National Council for Research; a travel-to-collection grant by *Tulsa Studies in Women's Literature*, which allowed me to read Eliot Bliss's diaries at the McFarlin Library, assisted by its rare book room staff who made my stay and my research a pleasure; and a grant by the University of Trieste which paid for cleaning and restoring Bliss's manuscripts.

I am especially indebted to all the librarians I had met and been helped by during my long search, who enabled me to consult the precious resources of libraries and rare book rooms both in Europe and the United States – in particular the whole staff at Bobst Library (New York University), the head librarian at the Syracuse University Library Special Collections for her help with "The Horace Gregory Collection", and the librarians at the University of Trieste and the University of Venice.

I also owe many thanks to friends and colleagues, first and foremost Jacqueline Bishop, who read the manuscript and offered their precious advice. Thanks to Amanda Perry, Isis Semaj-Hall and Allyson Latta for their suggestions and useful editorial comments. Sincere gratitude to Erin MacLeod, who saw the possibilities of my project, and all those at the University of the West Indies Press who helped make this book a reality.

A last word of thanks to my husband and my son, whom I dragged all around the world on Eliot Bliss's trail, and who often had to console me when I felt depressed and my research seemed to lead nowhere; they were there for me, accepting the fact that my free time was too often devoted to Eliot and Patricia. I like to think, however, that deep down they did enjoy the journey as much as I did.